Escape from Monticello

From

Monticello

By Steven K. Smith

MB3 Press

For more information, contact us at:

MyBoys3 Press, P.O. Box 2555, Midlothian, VA 23113

www.myboys3.com

Second Printing

ISBN: 978-1-947881-11-2

To Matthew,
for all your journeys ahead

ESCAPE
FROM
MONTICELLO

CHAPTER ONE

The clanging bars echoed across Cell Block 8. It was nearly lights out. Soon the desperate quiet would settle in, like it did every night, across the dozens of six-by-eight concrete living quarters for those deemed unfit for regular society.

Hollow's Ridge was medium security, which meant that inmates had the run of the courtyard during the day, could make trips to the prison library, could work a trade in the woodshop and laundry facilities, and were even escorted out along Route 10 for trash pickup every other month. It could be worse, but it wasn't good. And it was certainly not anywhere the men wanted to be. Some stayed for months, others for years or even decades, but it was never really home. For their bodies, perhaps, but not their hearts.

Ben was no different. He'd been busted six months ago for misdemeanor assault after getting picked up during a fight at Lucy's Roadside Tavern. A heated discussion had quickly escalated into a full-blown brawl. If it had been his first offense, Ben would have gotten off with a slap on the wrist, some community service, and a fine. But this wasn't his first offense. He'd been in and out of places like Hollow's ever since he was a kid. After his mom died and his dad gambled and drank away most of their money, Ben had been sent to live with his aunt. But she'd finally given up trying to keep him on the rails, and when he turned twelve, Ben landed in juvie. You could have made a solid argument that the deck had been stacked against him—that he'd never gotten a fair shake in life—and you'd probably be right. But he also knew he'd had plenty of opportunities to make the right choices, and too often he'd settled for the easy path.

Now, it had taken him three weeks to decide to make the right choice, but all that time, something was eating at him. Probably his conscience, if he still had such a thing. So here he was, standing at the pay phone outside the cell block captain's office. This was his chance to do right, even if only in a small way. This was his chance to help someone out who might need a hand.

As fate would have it, Ben had been filling in for Manny on custodial duty next to the small room with stacks of books, magazines, and the three online terminals that composed the Hollis McGregor Memorial Library. That was where he'd first seen the man, poring through books and hunched over the computer. No matter what time Ben went past the library, the man was there. Ben normally wouldn't be caught dead in a library and probably couldn't have located one growing up if he'd tried, but it was hard not to notice the man since he stuck out like a sore thumb. Ben also wasn't sure who Hollis McGregor was, but he must have loved books, and more than likely would have approved of Ben's "information gathering" while he emptied wastebaskets.

Ben wasn't sure if there was a "typical" inmate, but if there was, this guy certainly didn't look like him. His arms were clean of any ink or scars, and he had an almost professorial look about him. Manny thought the man was a teacher, or was it a historian? Ben couldn't quite remember. But either would explain why he seemed strangely at home in the book stacks. Ben didn't know why a historian would be locked up in the pen, but he was pretty certain the straight-laced guy couldn't kick-start a Harley, let alone ride with the Ghosts along the Blue Ridge. Millburn, Manny had said his name was, Jerry Millburn.

One afternoon, Ben glanced over the man's shoulder at the computer as he pushed by with his cleaning cart. The screen showed some kind of online bookstore, and from the looks of the weathered brown covers and bindings in the pictures, old books at that. With most inmates at Hollow's, Ben would have known to keep to his own business, but this guy didn't seem overly threatening.

"Shoppin' for books?" Ben said casually, more out of curiosity than anything else.

Jerry turned around, sizing Ben up carefully. There was a tedious, methodical way that he went about things.

He seemed to relax when he saw Ben was just cleaning up. Despite his clean-cut look, there was a fire in his eyes that made Ben think there might be more to this man than initially appeared.

"Something like that," Jerry replied.

"I'd a figured there'd be enough old books in here to do ya," said Ben, glancing at the stacks around them. How anyone could read all those words, let alone write them, was beyond his understanding. But maybe this guy was particular about things, just as Ben had a special preference for the custom handlebars on his bike.

"These are rare books," said Millburn. "Collectibles, actually. Something I was working on before I ended up in here."

"They valuable?"

The man nodded. "Quite."

Ben whistled. "Well, for your sake, I hope they deliver. Kind of hard to make pickups from here in the joint, no?"

Jerry grunted. "I'm getting out in a few weeks, thankfully. Until then, I've got someone on the outside taking care of things for me. Putting things in motion, if you will."

"Nice. Part of your crew?"

Jerry chuckled. "Something like that. Let's just say I've got an old score to settle."

Ben grinned and set down his broom. "All right, now we're talking." That was something he could get behind.

He had some definite plans to stop by the roadhouse whenever he got out of here.

"There's a few kids out there that are too smart for their own good," Jerry added.

Ben laughed. Kids were one headache he didn't have to worry about yet. As far as he knew, at least. He leaned against his pushcart. Talking to this lightweight was easier than cleaning up, as long as there weren't any guards watching.

"How many you got? They teenagers? My sister has five of 'em and those little buggers are nothing but trouble. Wouldn't be surprised if they end up in here too, to be honest with you."

Millburn shook his head. "I've got one, but these aren't mine. Like I said, just a score that needs to be settled."

Ben lowered his eyebrows. "With kids? How'd you get in trouble with some kids? They put you in here or somethin'?"

Jerry groaned and proceeded to fill him in on how three industrious kids had wronged him on the hunt for a historical treasure. "I don't care how old they are," he said, finally. "When I get out of here, they'll pay for what they've done to me."

Ben had quickly recognized Millburn's description of the two brothers and the girl. Even in the short time he'd been riding with the Confederate Ghosts biker gang, he'd heard about three not-so-ordinary kids that Luke "Mad Dog" DeWitt had taken a liking to. He talked about them like they were his own grandkids, though as far as Ben knew, they weren't.

Now as Ben stood at the pay phone, he almost hung up and walked away. But he didn't. A stilted, metallic ring came through the line.

A kid's voice answered.

"Hello?"

The operator's words cut through the earpiece.

"I have a collect call from Hollow's Ridge Prison for Sam or Derek. Do you accept the charges?"

CHAPTER TWO

S am's back hurt. His arms hurt. He pulled off the tan leather glove and brushed his hand through his sweat-matted hair. Brown mulch dust flew off and made him sneeze.

Derek set down the pitchfork and wiped sweat from his brow with the bottom of his T-shirt. "How much is he paying us to do this?"

Sam stared at the never-ending pile of brown wood mulch at the corner of Mr. Haskins' driveway and sighed. "He didn't say."

Derek frowned. "It better be a lot. This afternoon on the river couldn't come soon enough."

Sam would rather be at the river too, instead of shoveling his old neighbor's mulch. Actually, he could think of a lot of things he'd rather be doing. They'd filled the flowerbeds all along the front of the house, which seemed to be the most important part, but there were still three long areas in the back that needed filling. Sam didn't know why those needed mulch anyhow. The only visitor he'd ever seen at his neighbor's house was the mailman, and no one ever went in the backyard.

Mr. Haskins came around the side of the house and banged dirt from his boot treads on the first step of the wooden deck. "Thanks for the work, boys. I take back all those bad things I've said about you. Well, most of them, anyway. You just might be worth keeping around after all." He handed them each a tall glass of water. "But ya gotta stay hydrated. It won't do me any good to have you drop from heat exhaustion."

Sam took a glass and gulped down half the water. The late-summer Richmond morning was already humid. He shielded his eyes from the sun and took another drink. "Are we almost done?"

"Sam has a hot date on the water this afternoon," said Derek.

Mr. Haskins raised his eyebrows. "That right?"

Sam shook his head. "We're going to the park along the river for a picnic with Caitlin and her parents." He shot Derek a glare. "You'll be there too, stupid."

"Just to supervise."

Mr. Haskins patted Sam's shoulder. "Since you two are already on a break from the flowerbeds, I need your help for a few minutes in the garage."

They followed him to a detached garage that was hidden behind a group of trees at the start of his drive-way. They'd been inside Mr. Haskins' house several times to say hi, and in his yard even more to retrieve their baseball when it went over the fence, but never in the garage. Like everything else around the property, it was old, with faded and chipped paint. Mr. Haskins tugged on one of the double doors along the front. It looked like it might fall off its hinges if the wind blew too hard.

Just inside the opening sat an old car. Or at least that's what Sam thought was under the thick layers of dust. A blue tarp covered the windshield, and it didn't appear to have seen the road for quite a while.

"Like my ride?" Mr. Haskins chuckled. "Believe it or not, she used to go pretty fast."

Derek pointed to a red stripe on the side panel. "Were you a drag racer?"

Sam tried to picture Mr. Haskins in a racing suit and helmet zipping around a track.

"Drag racing?" The old man chuckled. "Nah, didn't race her, but she was a real lady magnet. In fact, it's what I was driving when I met Mrs. Haskins. She thought I was quite the catch." His eyes turned glassy as he stared at the car. "Married for fifty-three years, we were."

Sam thought he remembered hearing that Mrs. Haskins had died a couple years before they'd moved in next door. He suddenly felt bad for not coming over to talk to their neighbor more often. It must be lonely living all alone. Mr. Haskins was a little strange, but he was a nice old man.

"Julia would've liked you two. She had a way of putting up with troublemakers." Mr. Haskins grinned slyly. "Probably why she put up with me for so long." He looked up quickly. "But that's not why we're back here, is it?"

Derek glanced at the time on his phone impatiently. "Why *are* we back here, Mr. Haskins?"

The old man ignored Derek's tone and stepped around the car toward the back of the garage. "Need your help moving a few of these boxes out of here." He pointed to tall stacks of faded cardboard leaning against the wall. There were dozens. "Think you can do that?"

Derek muttered something under his breath but stepped up surprisingly fast and grabbed a box. He turned to Sam. "Come on. The quicker we do this, the quicker we get out of here."

They took turns carrying the dusty boxes to the front of the garage, laying them out next to each other near the door. When nearly half the boxes were piled along the front of the garage, Sam paused at the sound of a car stopping in the cul-de-sac. He grinned when he saw Caitlin jump out of her mom's white SUV. They were saved.

"I've never been so happy to see her in my life," said Derek.

Sam thought she wouldn't be coming over until lunchtime to go to the river, but it must have been later than he'd thought. He took a few steps up the driveway and called her name as the car pulled away.

"Hi, guys!" Caitlin called as she walked toward them up the driveway. "What are you doing?"

She started to give Sam a hug but stopped when she saw how dirty and sweaty he was. "Oh. Never mind. Hi, Mr. Haskins."

"We were just finishing helping with the mulch," explained Sam.

Mr. Haskins raised his eyebrows. "Finishing? You think just because she's here, you can leave?"

"Come on," Derek moaned. "We need a break."

Sam turned back and gave the old man a pleading look.

Mr. Haskins nodded at Caitlin. "What do you think, young lady? Should I let 'em call it a day?"

"They do look pretty tired," said Caitlin, smiling. "It's probably enough for one morning, don't you think?"

Mr. Haskins scratched his chin. "Aw, I suppose you've earned a break. Guess that mulch isn't going anywhere. I'm trying to teach these young bucks some work ethic."

"That'll take a while." Caitlin giggled and winked at Sam.

Oh brother. Sam shook his head. "Well, we should go."

Caitlin noticed the rows of old boxes behind them in the garage. "What's all that stuff?"

"Just a bunch of junk," Sam answered.

Mr. Haskins chuckled. "The remains of several previous missions to clean out this garage. Aborted missions, unfortunately, more times than I can remember. Thought I'd try to get it sorted out so I can have a sale to end all sales and get rid of this junk, as Sam calls it."

Caitlin stepped over to the boxes then glanced back at Mr. Haskins. "You mind if I look?"

"Have at it. I need to go through it all, anyway. Separate the diamonds from the rough. Who knows what could be in here?"

"Don't you?" asked Derek.

"I've probably forgotten more than you can remember, boy. You get to my age and you're just thankful to make it out of bed."

Some of the boxes Sam had carried were open. They seemed to be an odd mixture of car parts, clothes, and *National Geographic* magazines.

"Hey, books!" Caitlin called excitedly. "Oh, my mom would have a field day here."

Mrs. Murphy ran a bookstore on Monument Avenue in downtown Richmond. Caitlin worked there sometimes after school, running the register and helping shelve books. Sam had helped a couple times too, and it was actually fun.

She held up a hardcover with a dusty cloth spine. "*The Adventures of Tom Sawyer*! That's a classic."

"I used to read that one when I was about your ages," said Mr. Haskins. "Reminds me a little of you three."

"How's that?" asked Sam.

"It's filled with adventure and trouble."

"Were these all your books?" asked Caitlin.

"Nah, my wife's mostly. Some old ones too, I think. Julia's father taught at Virginia for many years. Most of them were his."

"You mean UVA?" Caitlin's eyes lit up again. "The University of Virginia?"

Mr. Haskins nodded. "Yep, Mr. Jefferson's university, Julia used to call it. She always meant to go through all those books, maybe display them somewhere proper..." He stared over Caitlin's head at the car in his garage for a moment. "Guess she never got around to it. I keep meaning to do it myself but somehow haven't found the time."

Sam felt another twinge of sadness. It seemed like Mr. Haskins would have all kinds of time living alone in this house, but maybe, just like the car, he couldn't bring himself to get rid of memories of his wife.

"Would you mind if I showed them to my mom?" asked Caitlin. "I mean, if that's not overstepping. I'm sure they mean a lot to you. Her bookstore sells a lot of rare books. They might be worth something."

Mr. Haskins bobbed his head, like he was weighing the offer, and then waved his hand, a smile filling his face. "Have at 'em."

"Are you sure?"

"Absolutely. Julia would want them to be looked after. They're not doing anyone any good in here."

Caitlin smiled. "Thanks! We'll pick them up when Mom comes to get me later."

"Sounds like a plan." Mr. Haskins pointed to the mulch pile up the driveway. "Now get out of here, boys, before I put you back to work."

Sam and Caitlin followed Derek back to their house. "Do you really think those books are valuable?"

Caitlin shrugged. "Maybe. My mom'll check them out. She's like us. She loves discovering things from history."

Since she'd started joining their adventures, Caitlin had proved herself a valuable part of the team. She was great at research and enjoyed exploring treasures from the past as much as he and Derek did. As a group, they seemed to have a knack for finding things that others didn't.

CHAPTER THREE

As Caitlin had suspected, her mom had been very interested in the books. She'd listed a few early editions she'd been able to quickly identify on some online buying forums, but there was still a lot more research and sorting to do. A few days later, Sam's dad dropped Sam and Caitlin off at the store on his way to a meeting. The bookstore hadn't yet opened, but Mrs. Murphy was already there doing some work. She pointed at the two remaining boxes of books from Mr. Haskins' garage.

"You two can work on those upstairs in the office while I straighten things up down here," Mrs. Murphy said. The "closed" sign still hung on the door at the front, and the aisles of books were dark.

"Thanks, Mom." They each picked up a box, and Caitlin directed Sam up the stairs into a bedroom-sized office. She switched on the lights and set her box on one of the two wide tables along the wall, motioning for Sam to do the same. "This should work."

Sam peeked through the blinds on a window that faced down into the store. It looked creepy without all the lights on.

"Okay, let's see what we've got." Caitlin pulled a handful of the old books from the first box and stacked them on the table. "I'm not sure if Mom's gone through these yet." A cloud of dust flew from the pile as it hit the table, and Sam sneezed loudly.

Caitlin looked over at him in mock disapproval. "At least turn away from the books, Sam. Nobody is going to want a book with your snot all over it."

"Right," Sam muttered, pulling a stack from his box with a little more care so dust didn't fly everywhere. He was interested to see what was in Mr. Haskins' old collection, but he knew Caitlin well enough to expect she'd likely take over the entire operation. If he didn't let her get under his skin, they'd get along fine. Kind of like Derek. Maybe good friends and siblings were just like that.

Sam looked at the first book on the pile. *The Complete History of Beekeeping.* Not exactly what he'd imagine would be a hot seller on the rare books market, but who knew? Maybe other things than the title determined the value of books. "This is a little like sorting through baseball cards."

"Do you collect those?"

"A little. My dad has some from when he was a kid, and he let Derek and me go through them."

"It's probably similar," agreed Caitlin. "What determines the value of cards?"

"A bunch of things, really. The age, the condition, how good the player was, of course." Sam tried to remember what else his dad had explained to them. "Oh, and also if the card is rare, or if there is some weird thing wrong with it."

Caitlin lowered her eyebrows. "What would be wrong with it?"

"Like if they misspelled the name, or listed him on the wrong team or position. But Dad's most valuable card is a Tom Seaver rookie card. He keeps it locked up, but he told me once that it was worth over a thousand dollars."

"Wow. That's a lot for a card."

"Rookie cards are the best."

"That does sound like books," said Caitlin. "Mom said first editions are the most valuable. Those are the oldest, made when a book was printed the very first time. It's a book's rookie card!"

Sam opened the cover of the beekeeping book and looked for a date like would be on the back of a baseball card. "Printed in the United States of America, copyright 1945." He looked up. "That's pretty old, I guess."

Caitlin glanced at his book and chuckled. "But I don't know how many people care about beekeeping. And that looks pretty worn." She reached over and turned a few pages. "See how the paper's yellowed and is coming loose from the binding?"

Sam nodded. "Yeah."

"That's not good."

"Got it." Sam set the bee book to the side and went through his stack. Some were historical textbooks about World War I, ancient Greece, or political philosophy. Others were novels that Sam had never heard of, and most of them were pretty beat up. He leaned back in his chair and glanced through the blinds down into the store, but it seemed boring down there too. Mrs. Murphy sat at the register counter punching numbers into a calculator. Maybe he should have just stayed home and helped Mom paint the bathroom.

"This is interesting," said Caitlin, pulling another book from her pile. It looked different from the ones Sam had inspected. It was smaller, like a notebook.

Sam edged forward to see it. "What is it?"

Caitlin gently opened the cover. "I'm not sure. The cover feels like a journal, but look, some of the pages are glued in, almost like a scrapbook."

There was handwriting inside, written in small, careful cursive like someone had taken great care with their words.

"'To Cornelia,'" Caitlin read. "'I have longed to write to you, dearest sister, for some time.'" She glanced down to the bottom. "Look, it's signed, 'Believe me to be yours most sincerely and affectionately, E.W. Randolph.'"

She flipped through some pages, then looked up at

Sam with wide eyes. "It's letters between two sisters. They've pasted them into this journal."

"Cornelia and E.W.?"

"I think so." Caitlin slowly turned the pages, careful not to rip the old paper. "I wonder who they were? This looks old."

Sam tried to look interested, but a journal between two girls wasn't that exciting to him.

Suddenly Caitlin gasped.

"What is it?"

"Look here." She pointed to a line near the top of a page in the middle of the book. "What number does that look like to you?"

He leaned toward the spot Caitlin pointed. The fancy cursive was hard to distinguish. "April 27…" He squinted and tried to read the rest, but it was smaller than the other parts. "1828?" He looked up from the page. "Could that be right? 1828? That *is* old."

Caitlin's eyes were wide. "It sure is." She flipped ahead and then squealed. "Oh my gosh, Sam. Listen to this." She moved her finger lightly across the page and read.

"Today I stepped through the dome. It feels so different from when we used to play there as girls. My heart longs for the days of old when Grandpapa used to teach and read to us there. My trips with him to Poplar Forest."

Caitlin stopped reading and looked up. "Does that sound familiar?"

"Grandpapa? I don't know anyone who talks like that."

"No, Poplar Forest!" She rolled her chair across the office and logged into her mom's laptop. She typed quickly into the search bar, then stopped, motionless.

"Well? Did you find anything?" Caitlin was probably his best friend, but sometimes she could really be confusing.

She nodded, but didn't speak. So Sam walked behind her to see the computer screen. Highlighted in the search results was a picture of an old brick house. He glanced down to the description.

Poplar Forest - Thomas Jefferson's retreat home.

He looked up in surprise. "Whoa."

CHAPTER FOUR

Caitlin grabbed the laptop and rolled her chair back to their table with the books. She turned the journal pages with giddy excitement.

Sam tried to piece things together in his mind. "So what does that mean? That the journal belonged to Thomas Jefferson?"

"No, but to someone in his family, I think." She typed a few more words into the search box. "See, it says right here. C.J.R.—Cornelia Jefferson Randolph, sister of Ellen Wayles Randolph. They were Thomas Jefferson's granddaughters!"

"I wonder if that makes it valuable."

"Valuable?" Caitlin stared at Sam like he had a hole in his head. "Just think about who this is from! There's only one Thomas Jefferson. You know, the writer of the Declaration of Independence?"

Sam rolled his eyes. Sometimes she made it hard to be

excited when she got so over the top about things. "Yes, I'm familiar with who Thomas Jefferson is, remember?" They'd worked through a mystery in Church Hill that had included a letter from Jefferson to his law professor, George Wythe. But this wasn't a letter from Jefferson. It was just something from his granddaughters. Probably about knitting or something boring.

Caitlin seemed to think letters between sisters were a lot more glamorous than they were. He and Derek didn't write letters to each other, but even if they did, it didn't seem likely that anyone would clamor to read them a hundred years from now. Then again, he supposed if one of their parents or grandparents were famous like Thomas Jefferson, maybe people would. Did texts count as letters?

"Maybe your mom can sell it."

Caitlin frowned. "You're unbelievable. Just imagine what it would have been like to have Thomas Jefferson as your grandfather." Caitlin shook her head. "I, for one, think it's very cool to see what his granddaughters had to say. And this is more than just a friendly letter between sisters. I think they're talking about something important." She moved her finger back to the top. "Listen to this."

"I've long considered the stories that Grandpapa told us as girls—of his hasty retreat from our beloved Monticello over the rugged trail to Poplar Forest in advance of the Redcoats, and of the best silver and other valuables

hidden away by Martin. Do you recall his tales of his missing collection? Did it ever resurface?"

That part caught Sam's attention. "Retreating from Monticello from the Redcoats. The British?"

"It has to be."

"Did the British invade Monticello?"

Caitlin twirled a long strand of her hair like she did when she was deep in thought. "I can't remember." She looked at her computer. "We'll need to do more research."

Sam looked back at the journal. "And who's Martin? It says he hid silver and valuables. That sounds like a treasure!" Now that was exciting.

She lifted the book and dramatically turned away from him. As she flipped through the journal, a page pulled loose and drifted to the floor.

Sam leaned down to pick it up. "You dropped something."

"Oh, no!"

The page seemed blank, but when he flipped it over, he realized it was simply folded in half.

"Be careful, Sam. It could be two hundred years old."

He unfolded the sheet slowly, revealing more of the cursive writing like in the journal. "It's another letter." He read the top. *Dear Ellen*, it began. The bottom was signed, *Yours, C.R.* He handed it to Caitlin, knowing she'd be much more excited about it than he were.

She placed the paper on the table next to the journal, gently flattening the edges before reading aloud.

"You're very right that the valuables were hidden away out of fear that the danger which threatened Charlottesville would return. But don't you recall the legend that some was taken to the Forest, including Grandpapa's collection, and was never recovered? Remember Mother's stories about clues and hiding places?"

The old-timey language was a little confusing, but Sam thought he understood. Caitlin kept reading.

"I last placed the details in the loose brick of our nice little cuddy that became our haunt. Do you recollect the place over the parlor portico into which the dome room opened? Remember how, breathing through a broken pane of glass and some wide cracks in the floor, we took possession with the dirt daubers, wasps, and humble bees. We did not intend to give it up to anything but the formidable rats which had not yet found out our fairy palace."

"I think they hid something important in a dome room," said Caitlin, looking up from the page. "She called it their fairy palace. It sounds magical!"

Sam frowned. "I don't know about the bees and

wasps, but a secret hiding place for a lost treasure sounds good to me. Is that all it says?"

Caitlin shook her head. "There's a little more."

"Whether it remains there still, I know not, but I rejoiced at least for a time when we learned the whereabouts of his collection had not been entirely lost. I know we did begin those hunts as stories and games, but since he's left us, I've come to earnestly believe it still lies waiting to be found. My heart aches that we did not more carefully keep his dear collection close."

"We have to figure this out," said Caitlin.

Sam's imagination started running wild. They'd found valuable treasures before, but his excitement always grew with each discovery. There was a little bit of magic inside each new mystery they solved.

"Caitlin?" Mrs. Murphy's voice boomed next to them.

They both jumped in surprise at the sound coming from the intercom in the wall. Caitlin giggled and pushed the intercom button. "Yeah, Mom?"

"I need you to go down the street to Angelo's Market and pick up the catering tray for the book signing I'm holding this afternoon. Sam, can you help? Grab yourselves some lunch while you're there. I'm about to get on a phone call with the book distributor, and I might be a while."

Sam's stomach growled at the mention of food.

They'd been so wrapped up in reading, he hadn't even realized he was hungry.

Caitlin laughed. She always seemed to notice the sounds from his tummy. "Maybe we should take a break." She pushed the button on the intercom. "Okay, Mom."

Sam pointed to the journal and the loose letter. "Should we show these to her?"

"Good idea. She might know more about the dates."

They walked downstairs and over to the counter. "Mom, you have to look at this!"

Mrs. Murphy smiled but held up her finger, the phone already to her ear. "That's right, do you need my account number?"

"We can just show her when we get back," said Sam.

Caitlin kept the loose paper but placed the journal on the counter. "Look at this when you're done," she whispered.

Mrs. Murphy nodded as she continued to pore over the order forms spread out on the counter.

Caitlin tucked the paper carefully into her purse. "I want to study this more at lunch."

"Which way?" asked Sam as they walked out onto the sidewalk. He'd eaten at Angelo's once before and thought they had the best subs in town. He could already taste the sandwich piled high with ham, turkey, Muenster cheese, lettuce, tomato, onions, maybe even some avocado… it would be great.

"Two blocks down there."

Sam turned in the direction Caitlin was pointing, but

his gaze stopped on a dark blue car parked along the curb across the street. That wasn't a big deal—there were lots of cars zooming up and down Monument Avenue—but something about it caught Sam's attention. The driver had long, red hair that poked out from under a hat. The hat cast a shadow over their face, but they seemed to be looking right at him and Caitlin. He considered saying something to Caitlin but realized it would sound stupid. His imagination was probably just getting the best of him. When he got super hungry, he could hardly think straight.

"You coming?" called Caitlin. "Or are you gonna take the bus?"

"Huh?" Sam glanced up to see Caitlin several yards ahead of him on the sidewalk. "Oh, yeah, sorry."

He looked back toward the driver of the car, but a bus had stopped at a red light and was blocking his view. All he could see was the bumper and license plate.

GMLOGMD.

Everybody in Virginia seemed to have a personalized plate. He and Derek often played a game to decipher what they meant, but he didn't see any clear meaning to this one, unless the "MD" at the end meant it belonged to a doctor. He caught up with Caitlin and refocused on what toppings he'd pick for his sandwich.

* * *

THEY ATE before picking up the catering tray, and his sandwich was definitely worth the wait. He'd had them load it down with every fixing he could find. It was a masterpiece. He needed to ask his parents to bring him to Angelo's more often.

"Should we get you another one for the road?" joked Caitlin as they finished up lunch.

Sam frowned as he finished the final two bites. "It's good," he said with his mouth full.

Caitlin held the letter in her hands but had a faraway look in her eyes. "I wonder what they thought about growing up that way."

"Who?"

"Nelly and Ellie."

Sam was pretty sure he'd been paying attention, but he still didn't know what she was talking about. "Who?" he said again.

Caitlin sighed. "You know, Jefferson's granddaughters, Cornelia and Ellen. I'm going to call them Nelly and Ellie for short, like we were all sisters. Cute, huh?"

"I guess." Caitlin always made a bigger deal about siblings than he did. Mostly, he assumed, because she was an only child. If she had a brother like Derek around, she'd get over the fascination pretty quickly.

"It must have been like a dream to grow up living in Monticello."

"Have you been there?" asked Sam.

"Barely."

"What do you mean barely? Either you have or you haven't."

"I was there with my parents once on the way to one of my dad's photo shoots at the Greenbrier in West Virginia, but it was a long time ago. I don't really remember it. Believe it or not, I wasn't as interested in history back then." She leaned toward him, her palms pressed onto the table. Her eyes were wide with excitement. "We should go!"

"To a photo shoot?"

"No, to Monticello, silly. We need to figure out what collection of Jefferson's they're talking about. Maybe it's still there!"

"Don't forget the silver and the valuables," said Sam.

"Of course, it could just be a collection of bugs or something."

"Bugs?"

She nodded. "He was a scientist."

"I thought he wrote the Declaration of Independence?"

Caitlin smiled. "Yes, but that's not all he did. He also was governor, ambassador to France, the first secretary of state, the second vice president, and of course, our third president."

"Of course." Sam felt tired just thinking about it all.

"And, after he retired from public service," Caitlin added, "he founded the University of Virginia."

"He was busy."

She chuckled. "Ya think?" She slurped the last drop of

her drink. "When we get back to the store, I'll ask Mom if she can take us to Monticello. Maybe we'll find out more about Nelly and Ellie."

"And the treasure."

"Yes, and the treasure, Sam. Derek can come too."

Sam moaned. "Way to ruin a fun plan."

"Oh, come on. He's not that bad."

Sam folded up his sandwich wrapper. "You'd be surprised."

"And besides, we always search for things together, remember? We don't want to break up our team now."

"I guess." Sam always had to remind himself that despite being super annoying, Derek was clever at solving parts of their mysteries. He usually pushed on to find things they wouldn't otherwise. Someday it was going to get them killed or in serious trouble, but so far they'd managed to avoid anything terrible happening because of one of Derek's suggestions.

Caitlin glanced at her phone. "My mom called, and I didn't hear it. We'll see her in a minute anyway." She stood from the table. "Are you ready? We'll grab the catering tray on the way out."

Sam nodded. "Let's go."

CHAPTER FIVE

Ablock from the bookstore, Sam noticed the same blue car that had been parked across the street. If Derek was there he'd accuse Sam of being paranoid, and maybe that's just what it was. But Sam had the sneaking suspicion they were being watched.

"Walk faster," said Sam, shifting the bag with the food tray in his arms.

"Faster?" Caitlin chuckled. "You know the last time we raced, I beat you fair and square."

"No, I don't want to race." He nodded across the street discreetly. "Don't look, but I think that car's following us."

Caitlin stopped and pointed. "That blue car?"

Sam pulled her arm back. "I said *don't* look, Caitlin!"

"Oh, sorry. But why would it be watching us?"

"I saw it when we left the bookstore. It seems like the same—" He stopped mid-sentence at the sound of squealing tires. Just as they had approached, the car lurched away from the curb, its engine roaring. Another passing car slammed on its brakes and blared its horn as the blue car made a fast illegal U-turn in the middle of the street. It gunned the engine again, now racing back in Sam and Caitlin's direction.

"Look out!" Sam cried, dropping the tray and leaping toward the closest building. He glimpsed a wave of red hair blowing in the wind as the car buzzed by.

"Slow down, you maniac!" yelled Caitlin.

Sam bent down and picked up the food tray. The lid was still on, but the food inside was all disheveled. "Sorry," he muttered as he put it back inside the grocery bag.

Caitlin shook her head. "Maybe there's something with you and this street. Remember how Mad Dog nearly ran you down on his motorcycle when the Ghosts were rallying by the monuments?"

Sam frowned. That other time he hadn't been paying attention. He was paying close attention now—that was how he'd noticed the car in the first place. He peered down the street but the car was already out of sight. "Come on, let's go inside."

When they entered the bookstore, Mrs. Murphy walked over and handed Sam two crisp hundred-dollar bills.

"What's this for?" he asked.

Mrs. Murphy grinned. "Turns out there was some interest in your neighbor's books that you brought me."

"What do you mean, Mom?" Caitlin glanced up at the office.

"Well, I listed the ones I could identify on the used book marketplace. It turns out, a collector was very interested in a few of them. Like we discussed, that's half the profits for you to give back to your neighbor."

"Wow, thanks, I guess." Sam leaned over the counter where Mrs. Murphy had been talking on the phone. He nudged Caitlin. "Where's the journal?"

Caitlin shrieked. "Mom, you didn't sell him the journal I laid here, did you?" She rushed around the corner of the counter.

"What in the world?" Mrs. Murphy furrowed her brow. "No, I only sold a few early editions from the box. The *Tom Sawyer*, *Catcher in the Rye...*" She looked at Sam in confusion. "I thought you'd be pleased?"

"We set an old journal on the counter next to you before we left," he explained. "What happened to it?"

Mrs. Murphy put her hand to her chin. "I don't know. I saw you place something there, but I didn't have a chance to look at it. I was on the phone with the distributor. Is it missing?"

"Mom, this is important," said Caitlin. "We think the letters in that journal were written by Thomas Jefferson's granddaughters!"

"What?" Mrs. Murphy put her hand to her forehead like she was getting a migraine. "Well, why did you put it on the counter?"

Caitlin's face reddened. "I don't know, Mom. I was

going to show it to you, but you were on the phone. We have to find it!"

Sam tried to think. Whenever Derek and he lost things around the house, his mom had them walk back through their day. Most of the time, they found what they'd misplaced. "Where did you go? Exactly."

Caitlin waved her finger. "Great idea. Mom, retrace your steps."

"Okay…well, she came in while I was still on the phone with the supplier, so I had to put them on hold."

"She?" asked Sam.

Mrs. Murphy nodded. "Yes, a young woman. Older than you two, but maybe college-aged. She asked about the books I'd listed online. She wanted to buy them right away." Mrs. Murphy looked at Sam. "Most people pay by credit card these days, but she paid cash. That's how I got those hundred-dollar bills I gave you. Or what do kids call them now, Benjamins?"

Caitlin smacked her own forehead. "Mom, focus. What happened then?"

"Well, I asked her to wait while I walked up to the office to retrieve the books. I came back, she paid, and then she left. Nothing too complicated."

Sam closed his eyes. "She must have swiped it off the counter while you were in the office."

Caitlin looked up, dejected. "How could you, Mom?"

Mrs. Murphy sighed. "I'm so sorry, honey. I didn't realize you'd left it on the counter or that it was so important to you. I tried to call and let you know someone was here to buy the books, but you didn't answer your cell." She draped her arm around Caitlin. "I should have waited, I guess."

Caitlin shook her head. "It's not your fault."

Sam glanced out toward the street. "Was she a regular customer? Has she ever been in the store before?"

Mrs. Murphy shook her head. "I've never seen her before. Since she paid in cash, I don't have any information about her. She seemed in quite a hurry, so we didn't make a lot of small talk."

"We must have just missed her," said Sam.

"Maybe we passed her on the sidewalk," added Caitlin.

"You would have noticed her," said Mrs. Murphy. "She had the most striking red hair."

"Red hair?" Sam realized they hadn't even told Mrs. Murphy about the car. "Was she wearing a hat?"

Mrs. Murphy nodded. "Yes, now that you mention it. I guess that was a little unusual."

"What do you mean?" asked Caitlin.

"Well, it wasn't a typical baseball cap like most folks wear these days. It was a vintage fedora style, white with a wide brim, like they used to wear back in the day. I suppose they're making a comeback."

"The person in the car had red hair and was wearing a hat," said Sam, "although I couldn't tell what kind."

"We were almost run down on the sidewalk," said Caitlin.

"Where?" Mrs. Murphy cried. "At the market?"

"No, just around the corner." Caitlin pulled the food tray from the bag and handed it to her mom.

"Sorry it got a little messy," said Sam.

Mrs. Murphy put her hands on her hips. "I keep saying they need to post more speed limit signs around here. People forget how much foot traffic we have. Someone's going to get hurt."

"I think it was on purpose," said Sam. He explained how he'd seen the dark car watching them when they left. "I think it was a doctor." He recited the license plate.

Mrs. Murphy looked skeptical. "This girl seemed a little young to be a doctor."

"I just wish I hadn't set the journal on the counter," said Caitlin. "If only we'd seen her."

Mrs. Murphy snapped her fingers. "I don't know why I didn't think of this before."

"What?" asked Caitlin.

"I probably have her recorded." She pointed to a security camera mounted discreetly between two bookcases on the wall beside them.

"Can we see?" asked Sam.

Mrs. Murphy nodded. "The feed records to the cloud. We can access it on my laptop up in the office." They headed for the stairs when the phone rang. Mrs. Murphy waved her hands in the air. "It never stops! Caitlin, you know how to log onto my computer. Just go up and see if you can find it. I'll be up in a minute."

"Okay, Mom."

Sam followed Caitlin back to the office. "We can still

go to Monticello and explore around. The letter has enough to get us started."

Caitlin sighed. "I guess." She sat at the far desk and logged in to the computer. "I just can't believe that in the thirty minutes we leave the store, that's when someone came in to buy those books. It's almost like they planned it that way."

She opened up the security file and found the footage for the day. A grainy black-and-white video image appeared from the side of the store looking directly at the register.

Sam frowned. "I think your mom needs to upgrade her security equipment."

"She doesn't normally have shoplifters. This system was probably here when she took over the building." She fast-forwarded through the day. They saw Mrs. Murphy moving in hyper-speed back and forth from behind the counter a dozen times, like she'd had way too much coffee.

"Look, there's us!" exclaimed Sam, as the image changed to show Caitlin and him walking in and stopping at the register. "Keep going."

As they sped through the footage, they saw themselves walking out the door.

"That's when we left for lunch," said Caitlin, slowing the speed a bit. "It should be right after this."

She forwarded until the door opened and a person in a light-colored hat with dark hair walked up to the counter. In the black-and-white footage, he couldn't tell if the hair was red or not. Mrs. Murphy was still on the phone behind the counter.

"There," said Sam.

Caitlin played the video at normal speed.

"I can't see her face," Sam moaned. The angle of the camera and the hat were blocking a clear view. She stood at the counter for a moment until Mrs. Murphy walked out of the picture.

"This must be when Mom went to get the books," said Caitlin. "Look! There's the journal still sitting on the counter." They watched as the girl glanced toward the office and then leaned forward, stretching her arm across the counter. She picked up the journal, flipped through the pages briefly, and then slipped it into her jacket just before Mrs. Murphy returned.

"That thief!" Caitlin huffed. "She just reached over and snatched it."

Sam had to admit, it was a bold move to steal something right off the register counter in the front of the store. She must have noticed the weathered cover and taken an interest while waiting. "Maybe she'll turn around." They watched as the girl handed over the money. Mrs. Murphy seemed surprised, but she smiled as she took the cash.

The girl picked up the books and walked swiftly out the door. Could they see her face when she turned?

"Go back a second," said Sam.

Caitlin reversed the recording to when the girl turned for the door.

"Pause it there." The image froze. The girl had turned toward the camera, but it still wasn't a straight-on shot. They didn't have a good view of her face.

"Unbelievable," moaned Caitlin.

Mrs. Murphy walked up behind them and leaned down toward the monitor. "That's her, but you can't really see very clearly, can you?"

"No," said Caitlin.

"I suppose I need to get a new camera." She rested her hand on Caitlin's shoulder. "I'm sorry, honey. Should I call the police? I could report it as a robbery."

"I don't know. It will be hard to prove. It's a pretty grainy picture, and we have no idea who it was. Plus, we don't really have a great description of the journal." Caitlin carefully pulled the single yellowed piece of paper from her purse. "At least we still have this."

Sam explained what they'd figured out so far. "Do you know if Jefferson had a dome room?"

"I always think of the Rotunda at the university," said Mrs. Murphy. "It has a large dome. The UVA library also has a large rare books collection. If this is an important letter from Jefferson's granddaughters, they may have a record of it. After all, it's—"

"I know, Mom," Caitlin interrupted. "It's Mr. Jefferson's university."

Mrs. Murphy raised her eyebrows.

"Sorry." Caitlin sighed loudly. "I'm just angry. How could someone just steal something like that? It's not right!" She looked back at her mom. "Can you take us to the UVA library?"

Mrs. Murphy glanced up at the clock. "Not today, I'm afraid. I have to finish going through my order logs with the distributors before this afternoon's book signing. And tomorrow I'm the only one running the store, so I'll be busy."

"I'll bet my parents can take us tomorrow," said Sam. "They enjoy going places like that. I can check with them when I get home."

"Perfect," said Caitlin. She held open the letter and studied it again. "Now we just have to figure out what all this means."

CHAPTER SIX

"How far is it to UVA?" Derek asked from the back row of the van.

"Charlottesville is only about an hour from Richmond," answered Dad from the driver's seat.

Sam watched the stream of cars and tractor-trailers on the highway. "Thomas Jefferson probably made this trip a lot from Richmond to Charlottesville. Although it would take longer on horseback, I guess."

Mom laughed. "Just a bit."

"It reminds me of Jack Jouett," said Caitlin.

Derek poked his head over the back of the middle seat. "Who?"

Caitlin raised her eyebrows. "Don't you pay attention in social studies class?"

Derek chuckled. "Sometimes."

"He's like Paul Revere," explained Caitlin.

"I do know some things," said Derek, "and I'm pretty sure Paul Revere was in Boston."

"Right," said Caitlin, "but Jouett did something very similar in Virginia. He just didn't have a famous poem written about him, like Longfellow wrote about Revere."

"Don't feel bad, son." Dad glanced back at them in the rearview mirror. "I didn't know who Jack Jouett was, either."

"Honey!" Mom looked shocked. "Didn't *you* pay attention in school?"

"Right on, Dad," Derek called. "Slackers unite!"

Dad shook his head. "I *did* pay attention in class, thank you very much. But I don't think they taught about Jack Jouett in New York. We learned about the Battle of Saratoga though."

"Sara-hooga?" asked Derek.

Dad laughed. "Exactly. Sometimes where you live has a big influence on what you're taught."

"I suppose that's true," said Caitlin. "But what you learn is still up to you, Mr. Jackson."

Dad nodded. "Touché, Caitlin. Very true."

"Caitlin, why don't you tell us the story?" said Mom. "It sounds like we need to educate these boys."

Caitlin's eyes lit up as they always did when she got to show off her knowledge. She straightened in her seat and took on a serious expression. "Well, when Thomas Jefferson was governor of Virginia—"

"You mean president," interrupted Derek.

"No," said Caitlin. "Before that."

"I thought he wrote the Declaration of Independence before that?"

Caitlin sighed. "He did, but in between, he was governor of Virginia."

"Wow," said Derek.

Sam nodded. "That's what I said."

Caitlin folded her arms. "So anyway, Jefferson's term as governor was almost over, but the British were advancing on the capitol in Richmond under the command of Benedict Arnold."

Derek held up a finger. "He did something bad, didn't he?"

"Yes, he was a turncoat. He defected to the British and then led their army against ours," said Caitlin.

"Saratoga!" Dad exclaimed.

Sam looked up at him. "What?"

"Benedict Arnold. He won the Battle of Saratoga before he turned." Dad smiled at Mom. "See, I told you I paid attention."

"Maybe." Mom patted him on the shoulder. "Let's let the girl finish her story, honey."

"Thanks," said Caitlin. "So Governor Jefferson and the legislature left the state capital and fled to Charlottesville."

"Like us," said Sam, glancing back at the highway.

"We're not exactly fleeing, Sam," said Derek.

"Did they meet at the university?" asked Mom.

Caitlin shook her head. "No, this was before that. But Charlottesville was where Jefferson lived at—"

"Monticello!" shouted Dad.

Mom shook her head. "Honey."

"Very good, Mr. Jackson."

Dad smiled wide. "Thanks, Caitlin."

Sometimes Sam wondered if Dad was as goofy as a boy as Derek was now. They certainly seemed to have that trait in common sometimes.

"So British troops were sent to capture Jefferson and the legislature in Charlottesville," continued Caitlin. "But luckily, Jack Jouett overheard them talking at the Cuckoo Tavern."

"Cuckoo?" asked Derek.

"You're just making this up now," said Sam.

Caitlin held up her hands. "No, it's true. That's what it was called, the Cuckoo Tavern."

Derek leaned against the middle seat. "I want to see this place. Can we stop there?"

"I don't know if it's still standing," replied Caitlin.

"How convenient." Derek started making sounds like those clocks where the bird jumps out on the chimes. "Cuckoo, cuckoo!"

"So *anyway*," said Caitlin. "Jouett knew he had to alert Jefferson and the legislature, so he rode on back roads for forty miles by the light of the moon to Charlottesville to warn them."

"Huh," said Sam. "That *is* a lot like Paul Revere."

"Did he yell, 'The British are coming!'?" asked Derek.

"Maybe," said Caitlin, laughing.

"Did he make it?" asked Dad.

"He sure did," said Caitlin. "And they got away just in time."

Sam thought back to what they'd read in the bookstore. "Isn't that what the journal was talking about? The granddaughters said he'd had to flee Monticello?"

For maybe the first time ever, Caitlin didn't answer. Sam noticed her face had turned bright red. "Didn't you think about that?"

"I, uh," she stuttered, then looked out the window. "I don't want to talk about it."

"But that's it, right?" asked Sam, trying to piece together things in his mind.

Mom turned and gave him a glance that said *take it easy*. "Sam, if it is, let's not rub it in."

Sam was still marveling over making a connection about history before Caitlin did, when loud music broke out from the seat behind them. It was the theme song from *Jurassic Park*. Derek had made it his ringtone ever since they'd worked with the archeologists at Jamestown. He quickly pulled out his phone and answered it.

"Jay, what's up?"

As Derek chattered away on his phone call, Sam nudged Caitlin's arm. "Sorry."

She let out a deep sigh and reluctantly looked back at him. "It's okay. I just feel stupid. I've been making a lot of bonehead moves lately, like leaving the journal on the counter to get stolen. I don't know what's wrong with me."

He held back the temptation to gloat. "You're not

stupid. It's all good. And we still have the letter. I think that's the important part anyhow."

She gave him a weak smile. "Thanks."

As they pulled up to the campus, there were students walking everywhere. A huge banner read: *Congratulations 2019 Men's Basketball National Champions. Go Wahoos!*

"Wow, that's cool," said Derek. "I wonder if I could make that team someday."

"I didn't think you played basketball," said Caitlin.

"I could be a walk-on," said Derek.

"You could be the mascot," said Sam. He could easily picture his brother dressing up in one of those costumes and acting stupid. He did that now without a costume.

Dad found a parking space along University Avenue. They walked up the sidewalk toward a stately brick building with half a dozen columns, but it was the white-domed roof that caught his attention. "Is that the Rotunda?"

Caitlin nodded. "Isn't it beautiful?"

"It looks like something in Washington, DC."

"Thomas Jefferson loved architecture."

Sam looked over at his parents. "Can we go in?"

"Of course," said Mom. "That's why we're here."

They walked beneath the columns and through the entranceway. A few important-looking rooms were to the side of the hall, but it didn't look the same as it had from the outside. "Where's the dome?"

"I think the good stuff's up here," said Derek, already bounding up the staircase.

They followed him to the second floor and soon were standing at the edge of a huge, circular space. White columns and a balcony wrapped around the edges of the room, with chairs and small workspaces behind the railing. Students were dotted throughout the room, studying quietly.

Sam pointed up at the circular window in the center of the white-domed ceiling. "It's like a skylight."

As they stared at the ceiling, a group of prospective college students and their parents gathered around a young tour guide.

"We can listen in!" Caitlin whispered.

"The Rotunda building is the centerpiece of our grounds," explained the guide. "Jefferson modeled it after the Roman Pantheon. The university was founded in 1819; however, this building was still unfinished at the time of Jefferson's death seven years later. The size and shape of the room has been altered many times since Jefferson's day, but during the nation's Bicentennial in 1976, much of it was returned to the original designs."

Caitlin glanced at the boys. "That was America's two-hundred-year birthday."

Derek gave her an "of course I knew that" look.

"Jefferson also designed the lawn and the surrounding area, which he called the Academical Village," said the guide.

Sam tried to picture what it would be like to go to a school founded and designed by Thomas Jefferson. Did the students appreciate it, or did it just become normal after a while like most things?

As the tour moved on, the kids walked back outside ahead of Sam and Derek's parents.

"That was a dome," said Sam, when they were back on the lawn, "but it doesn't match the letter's description."

Caitlin nodded. "You're right. It doesn't look like a fairy palace."

Derek made a face. "Did you say 'fairy palace'?"

"Just focus on the treasure part," said Sam. They may have left out a few details when they'd filled Derek in about the letter. The same way they had left a few details out when telling the story to their parents.

"We can ask in the library," said Caitlin. "Maybe they can help us find the right dome."

Sam didn't see any other domes near the grassy lawn. The surrounding buildings were laid out in a U-shaped design. "Is this what the guide was talking about, the Academical Village?" He'd never heard anyone use those words together like that.

Before Caitlin could answer, Derek waved over two male students who were walking by on the sidewalk.

The first guy pulled out his earbuds and looked up. "Yeah?"

Derek pointed to the buildings around the lawn. "Is this where the freshman dorms are?"

The boy shook his head. "Lawn Rooms are only for fourth years."

"You mean seniors?" asked Caitlin.

"Basically. We don't call them freshmen or seniors. We say first, second, third, and fourth years."

"How come?" asked Derek.

"Beats me."

The second student smacked the first guy's head. "It's from Jefferson, stupid."

"Oh, right, it's from Jefferson."

Caitlin laughed. "That seems to be the answer to most things around here."

"Pretty much," said the second guy. "He said that you never stop learning, so that's how he named the years."

"Is it easy to get a Lawn Room?" asked Derek.

"No, it's super hard," said the first boy. "There's a whole application and selection process."

"Some famous students have lived there though," said the second guy. "Edgar Allen Poe, Katie Couric…"

"Who?" asked Derek.

"Never mind," interrupted Caitlin as the boys' parents walked down the steps from the Rotunda. "Thanks for the info."

"Did you find that interesting?" asked Mom.

"Oh, yeah," said Derek, a wide grin across his face. "But now I think it's about that time."

"I'm afraid to ask," said Dad.

"About what time?" said Mom, raising her eyebrows.

"It's time for you to do all your parent stuff and give us some space," said Derek.

Mom frowned. "I'm not sure if I'm ready to let you loose on a college campus yet."

"What are you talking about?" Derek held his hands out wide. "Remember how we stayed in the dorms at William & Mary for Field School at Jamestown? That was a college campus."

Sam had to give his brother credit—he wasn't afraid to ask for what he wanted.

"We'll just be in the library," said Caitlin. "We have some historical investigating to do."

Dad checked his watch. "Well, I did want to stop in at the business department to say hi to Bob Charles from the economic summit."

"How about we give you an hour," said Mom. "Then we can meet up for lunch."

"Sweet," said Sam. "Thanks."

"Just behave yourselves," said Dad.

"Dad," moaned Derek. "It's the *library*. How much trouble could we get in at the *library*?"

Sam held up his hand. "Don't answer that."

CHAPTER SEVEN

"Which way's the library?" asked Derek.

Sam opened the campus map he'd picked up in the Rotunda. "There's a few of them."

Caitlin leaned over his shoulder. "We need the rare books section. *Special Collections.* I'll bet that's it." She looked up and pointed away from the lawn.

They followed the system of crisscrossing sidewalks until they reached the building on the map. A girl at the entrance directed them downstairs past several rooms with rows of books, display cases, and artwork.

The hustle and bustle of the campus outside faded away. This seemed more like a museum. Sam looked ahead through a glass-partitioned wall with a door. "Are you sure we're allowed to be down here?"

Derek glared at him. "I'm going to get you a shirt with those words written on it so you can stop saying them, Sam."

Caitlin started laughing. "It's a library, Sam. This one's just where they keep the special books." She glanced quickly at Derek. "We can be here, as long as we're careful."

"Why are you looking at me?" Derek asked.

Caitlin pushed open the glass door and walked confidently up to the counter where two older women were sitting in front of computer monitors. "Hello," she said cheerfully.

One of the women looked up and smiled. "Hello there, children."

"Is this where you keep the rare books?" asked Derek, pushing ahead of Caitlin.

"Why, yes, it is. This is the Special Collections library. We have many original manuscripts and old texts."

"Great," said Derek. "That's what we need."

The woman raised her eyebrows and glanced down the dark wooden desk. Another woman came over to them. "What exactly are you looking for?"

Caitlin nudged Derek to be quiet. "What he means is, we're doing some very special research for our social studies class about Thomas Jefferson's granddaughters. Specifically, Nelly and—uh, I mean Cornelia and Ellen Randolph."

"Is that so?" The two women exchanged surprised glances. "Well, we do have a collection of documents that includes letters from Thomas Jefferson's grandchildren; however, those are very delicate," the second woman explained.

"Just point the way," said Derek.

The woman frowned. "I'm afraid it's not that simple."

"Don't you allow people to look at them?" asked Sam. Maybe important documents related to Thomas Jefferson were off-limits.

The woman paused, seeming to choose her words carefully. "Yes, they are available to look at."

"Is it because we're kids?" asked Derek.

She chuckled nervously. "That crossed my mind."

"We'd be very careful," said Caitlin. "We promise."

The woman smiled. "I'm sure you would, dear, but we have to be diligent in preserving our collection."

Derek leaned his elbows against the counter, flashing one of his best convincing smiles, the same kind he used with Mom and Dad when he wanted something. He stared at the second woman's name tag. "Listen, Martha. Do you mind if I call you Martha?"

She raised her eyebrows cautiously. "Sure…"

Derek smiled wider. "I totally understand your hesitation to let three kids get close to something so important. I mean, *I'd* probably be nervous about it if I were you, too." He glanced back at Sam. "Especially with my brother. I know he looks reckless."

Sam sighed and folded his arms.

"But the thing is," Derek continued, "we've had quite a bit of experience with stuff like this."

"Is that so?" asked Martha.

"Oh, sure. Do you know Professor Evanshade at the Virginia Museum?"

"William?"

Derek nodded. "Exactly. Doc and us go way back. We've worked together a lot recovering important items from history—old coins, historic documents, lost artifacts." He leaned a little closer. "It's kind of our thing."

Martha glanced at Caitlin, as if to confirm what she was hearing.

Caitlin nodded. "It's true. You can call him if you'd like."

The woman considered the idea for a moment but then looked back at them. "What exactly would you like to see?"

Caitlin carefully pulled the letter from a folder in her backpack. "We need to compare this letter to some other writings from Jefferson's granddaughters."

Sam didn't know if Martha was a historian or simply worked at the information desk, but as she studied the old sheet of paper, her jaw dropped open with surprise. It clearly wasn't what she'd expected. He wondered if she realized how old it was.

"And you got this letter where?"

"It fell out of a journal kept by two sisters," Sam said. "That's why we're looking for more information about them."

"May I see this journal?" asked Martha.

"Unfortunately, they lost it," said Derek.

"Lost it?"

Caitlin shook her head. "It was stolen, actually."

"We found it in our neighbor's garage, but someone

swiped it at the bookstore," said Sam. "It's kind of complicated. All we have left is this letter."

"But we're hoping you have something similar," Caitlin added, looking up at Martha with pleading eyes. "Please?"

Martha typed into her computer. "We do have a collection of letters between Jefferson's granddaughters." She paused and clicked a few more buttons. "That's interesting. It's currently checked out."

Sam's expression sank. "Someone took it?"

Martha shook her head. "No, we don't allow items like that to leave the library. They can only be viewed here in our reading rooms."

The other woman chimed in. "Actually, I pulled that item earlier for a student. She's still in the reading room, I believe."

Sam's eyes opened wide. "She is?"

"Can we talk to her?" asked Caitlin.

Martha shook her head. "I'm afraid we can't impose on a student who is already looking at one of our items, but if you'd like to look at it when she's done, I suppose we can arrange that. I'll need to supervise you, however."

"We're also trying to find the Dome Room," said Caitlin. "We walked through the Rotunda here on campus, but it doesn't look like it was ever a playroom for Jefferson's granddaughters."

"We're looking for a fairy palace," Derek said. "You don't happen to have one of those, do you?"

Martha smiled. "Why of course."

"You do?" asked Sam in surprise.

"Awesome," said Derek. "Where is it?"

"I'm afraid you're looking at the wrong dome," said Martha. "The one you want is not here on campus."

"It's not?" asked Sam.

"It's an easy mistake to make," explained Martha. "Jefferson was quite enamored with domes, but I think what you're looking for is at Monticello. There's a small nook off the Dome Room where his granddaughters used to play. It's called the Cuddy, I believe."

"Yes!" exclaimed Caitlin. "That's what they called it in the letter."

"Then I guess we have to go to Monticello," said Derek. He smiled again at Martha and Betty. "Thank you both so much."

"You're welcome," replied Martha. "That's what we're here for. It's nice to see children so interested in history."

They headed toward the exit, but when they were out of sight of the information desk, Derek turned down another hallway.

"Where are you going?" Sam asked.

"To the reading room. I want to get a look at this girl."

"Look at her?" asked Caitlin. "Why?"

Derek folded his arms. "Don't you think it's a little odd that on the day we come to look at the papers from Jefferson's granddaughters, someone else is doing the exact same thing?"

Sam thought for a moment. "Well, it is Jefferson's

university. I mean, the one he founded. People might do that every day."

"Martha seemed to think it was unusual," agreed Caitlin.

"Exactly." Derek stopped next to the reading room but pointed to the door of the room next to it. That room seemed to share a common glass wall with the reading room, although the door was marked "Staff Only." Derek cracked it open and peeked in. Then he turned back to Sam and Caitlin and nodded. "Come on. We can see in from here."

Sam was about to object, but Derek and Caitlin were already inside. He followed behind and moved past several desks to where Derek and Caitlin were crouched behind a long bookshelf as they peered through the glass into the next room. The reading room had an open floor plan with half a dozen rows of long desks, each with a light.

"What now?" Sam struggled to see around Derek's shoulder. The parts of the room that he could see were empty.

"There she is. Over in the corner." Derek pointed to the back.

Sam crouched lower and peeked through a space between the books to get a better view.

Caitlin nudged his arm. "Look at that!"

It was the first thing he'd noticed. A student sat at a table with her back to them. A student with red hair.

The girl huddled over a document, flipping slowly

through pages. She wore white gloves, presumably to protect the pages she was examining. They watched her periodically stop, jot something in a notebook, and then turn back to the document.

Sam couldn't see the girl's face, but he recognized what lay on the chair next to her. A white fedora-style hat. Just like in the security video. He turned and gawked at Caitlin.

"Do you think?" Caitlin said.

"What?" asked Derek.

"The girl from the bookstore had red hair and a hat just like that," whispered Sam.

"The one who stole the journal?"

Sam nodded.

"Is it her?" asked Derek.

"It's got to be," said Sam. "That would be one coincidence too many."

"What's she doing here?" asked Derek.

"Probably the same thing we are," said Caitlin. "Trying to get more information about the entry in the journal. But we have one thing that she doesn't." She patted her backpack where she'd stored the loose letter.

Maybe the information in the journal was even more important than they thought. Why else would the thief quickly visit the rare books library? There had to be something more.

"Now I really want to know what she's looking at," said Derek.

"We'll just have to wait till she's done," sighed Caitlin.

"Maybe we should introduce ourselves," said Derek. "I'll bet she'd be impressed that we're interested in history too. I have a way with the college ladies."

"Don't you remember?" asked Caitlin. "She's a thief. I don't want anything to do with her."

Suddenly, music erupted from Derek's pocket. They all jumped and then ducked further behind the bookcase. The ringtone from Derek's phone echoed even more loudly than usual in the dead quiet of the library.

"Will you shut that off!" Sam hissed.

"I'm trying," said Derek, reaching into his pocket. "It's Mom."

Sam turned back to the reading room. The glass partition didn't look soundproof. Surely the girl would have heard the music. He peeked back through an opening in the bookshelf.

The girl was staring right at him.

CHAPTER EIGHT

"What do you think you're doing back here?" a deep voice boomed from behind them.

Sam took his eyes off the red-haired girl in the reading room and spun around. A security guard with massive biceps was standing with his arms crossed at the end of the row of books, giving them the evil eye.

"Oh, hi!" Derek replied cheerfully. "Where were you when we needed you?"

"Excuse me?" said the man.

"My brother here, he, uh, lost a contact lens."

"Is that right?" He looked skeptical. "You kids shouldn't be back here."

Sam patted Derek on the shoulder. "I found it. Let's go."

"Oh, thank goodness." Derek smiled up at the man. "I tell ya, he's as blind as a bat without them. Ever since that incident with the snake-in-a-can."

The security guard glared down at them. "The what?"

Derek nodded and kept talking. "Yeah, you know those cans with a snake inside that jumps out and surprises you? I gave him one on April Fool's Day. It wasn't pretty."

Sam shook his head. There was no end to Derek's craziness.

Caitlin tugged on Derek's arm as she tried to stifle a laugh. "Come on. We have to meet your parents for lunch."

"I don't want to see you kids in here again," warned the guard, stepping to the side as they left the stacks.

"Yes, sir," said Caitlin.

Sam glanced back at the reading room, but the table where the red-haired girl had been sitting was empty. She was gone.

"What are we going to do now?" said Sam. "We needed to see that book."

"Do you really think it was the girl from the book-store?" asked Caitlin.

"It had to be," Sam answered.

Caitlin twirled a strand of her hair with her fingers. "Well, then this has all gotten a lot more complicated."

Sam blocked the sun with his hand as they walked outside. "Let's go find Mom and Dad. They won't believe it."

Derek placed a hand on Sam's shoulder. "Hang on, little brother."

"What now?"

"You know what I'm going to say."

Sam rolled his eyes. "Are you kidding me?"

"What's wrong?" asked Caitlin.

"We can't tell them yet," said Derek. "We need to get to the bottom of this. We don't even know for sure it's the same person. There's more than one redheaded girl in Virginia."

"It was her," Sam answered defiantly. He tried to picture her face. He hadn't recognized her, but it was almost like she recognized *him*. He turned back to Caitlin. "What do you think?"

"I think we need to go to Monticello and see the Dome Room. Whoever that was in the reading room, she doesn't have the letter, which means she doesn't know to look for the Cuddy."

"What if she's following us?" asked Sam. "Remember how she nearly ran us over with her car?"

Caitlin shook her head. "I can't give up without learning what Ellie and Nelly were talking about. If it's still out there, we have to find it."

Sam sighed in disgust. He was done asking Caitlin for her opinion. The more she hung out with them on adventures, the more she adopted Derek's daring attitude. "Fine," he mumbled. "Whatever."

"Did you find the library?"

Sam turned around to see his parents standing behind them. "Don't sneak up on me like that, Mom!"

"Everything all right?" asked Dad.

"Sure," answered Derek. "But we decided we need to head up to Monticello. Is that okay?"

Mom smiled. "We had a feeling you might say that."

"You did?" asked Sam.

"It's just up the hill," said Caitlin. "If we could, that would be perfect."

Sometimes Sam wondered if his parents had more of a clue about everything than he and Derek gave them credit for. He felt bad for making them worry over the situations he and his brother got themselves into, even if things had always worked out. At least so far.

"Great," said Derek. "Let's go."

"But maybe we should get some lunch first," said Mom.

"Sweet," said Sam. "I'm starving."

"That's what I'm putting on the back of the shirt," said Derek. "I'm starving."

Mom raised her eyebrows. "Shirt?"

Sam shook his head. "Don't worry about it, Mom."

On the way back to the parking lot, Sam spotted a familiar blue car at the curb. He leaned around to see the license plate. Just as he'd suspected: GMLOGMD. He nudged Caitlin and pointed at the plate. "See, I knew it was her. It's the same car as outside the bookstore."

"The doctor?"

"I don't know who she is, but she's not a doctor."

Derek looked where they were pointing. "Maybe she's a medical student."

"I think UVA has a med school," said Caitlin. "You could be right."

"But that still doesn't explain why she's here," said Sam. "Or why she stole the journal."

"Good men laugh over giant mouse droppings," Derek mulled. "Or, Grandma must love our great muddy dog."

"What?" asked Caitlin.

Derek laughed. "The license plate."

Sam shook his head. "You're nuts."

CHAPTER NINE

S am had never been to Monticello, but he'd assumed it would be a lot like George Washington's house at Mount Vernon. It seemed like they had preserved all the mansions and plantations of famous Founding Fathers and early presidents. Which was how it should be, he guessed. At least the preservation part. His teacher said that history was constantly being written, but Sam figured it would always be important to see where things started out.

Derek pointed to a colonial-looking building along the steep winding road. "Is that it?"

Mom shook her head. "That's Michie Tavern, but it's also from the late eighteenth century."

"Maybe that's where Jack Jouett stopped for a break on the way to warn Jefferson," said Sam.

"Good guess," said Mom. "But during Jouett's day, it was located twenty miles from here. They moved it piece by piece in trucks and wagons nearly a hundred years ago to this more populated area near Monticello." She nudged Dad. "I remember that from *my* class."

"They moved the entire place?" asked Derek. "Talk about cuckoo."

Sam noticed the busy parking lot and signs for a restaurant, gift shop, and artisan buildings. It was a smart idea to have something here with all the tourists heading to Jefferson's house.

About a mile further up the mountain, they turned in to a cluster of adjoining parking lots. Mom bought tickets and they boarded a shuttle bus.

"Most folks prefer to take this bus up the hill," explained the driver, "but on your way back you can take the path if you'd like. Mr. Jefferson's grave will be along the way." The shuttle stopped at a circular drive in front of Monticello. "Welcome to the little mountain," said the driver. "That's what *monticello* means in Italian."

"Thank you," said Mom as they exited.

"Wow, what a view," said Derek.

Sam stared across the valley. He could see why Jefferson had picked the spot for his house. You could see for miles.

"Look, I can see the Rotunda." Caitlin pointed between the trees at a group of buildings far below them that looked like the college campus.

"I wonder if Jefferson sat right here and imagined building a school down there," said Derek.

"I could imagine a lot of things up here," said Sam.

To the left of the house was a trail with several small buildings. Below them were gardens with plants and vegetables growing from the soil. A solitary gazebo-like pavilion overlooked the valley.

"*Mulberry Row,*" read Derek from an informational sign. "It says these were the houses and shops for over 130 slaves and laborers that worked the 5,000-acre plantation."

"It took a lot of workers to keep a big plantation like this running," said Dad.

"It's weird," said Caitlin.

"Are you talking about Sam again?" asked Derek.

"Stop, I'm being serious."

"What's weird, Caitlin?" asked Mom, frowning at Derek to be quiet.

Caitlin pointed across the acres of farmland and gardens around the mansion. "I don't know. It's just weird how Thomas Jefferson could write in the Declaration of Independence that 'All men are created equal,' and yet he owned slaves. How could he say that and still enslave so many people? I mean, owning another person is horrible. That's kind of hypocritical, isn't it?"

Dad nodded. "A good point, Caitlin."

"It gets even worse than that," said Derek, reading another sign. "It says here that they believe Jefferson had several kids with one of his slaves."

"Sally Hemings," said Caitlin.

Sam grimaced. "I'll bet his wife didn't like that."

"I think it was after his wife had died," said Mom.

Derek shrugged. "But still. That's kind of messed up."

"I'm afraid there are a lot of 'messed up' things in the world," said Dad. "I appreciate that you three love history, but most things aren't black and white. You'll discover this for yourselves as you get older. Human beings are complex. Jefferson had many great accomplishments, but he also made some huge mistakes."

"Kind of like some other families I know," Mom said.

"He's a contraption," said Derek.

"You mean a contradiction," said Caitlin, chuckling.

Derek grinned. "Right, that's what I meant."

"So what are you saying, Dad?" said Sam. "That there's no right or wrong, just shades of gray?"

Dad shook his head. "I think you know well enough that I believe in right and wrong, Sam. But I also know that we all do a bit of both. None of us are ever perfect. We all have weaknesses. Even someone like Jefferson."

"That's why history is so important," said Caitlin. "We can learn from it. Take the good things that Jefferson did and try not to repeat his mistakes."

"Precisely," said Dad.

Derek sighed. "Remind me to learn from my mistake of bringing up this subject. I thought we were going inside?"

Mom laughed and pointed to a bearded man walking toward them. "I think you're in luck."

"Are you all here for the next tour?" the man called to them.

"Yes!" answered Derek, running up the path that led to the tall columns on the front porch of the house.

As they moved closer, Sam noticed a small curved section of the roof above the porch. He nudged Caitlin. "Look, a dome."

"Now we just need to get inside," she whispered.

They gathered with a couple other families around the bearded tour guide named John. His name tag said he was a docent.

Sam tapped his mom's shoulder. "What's a docent?"

"It's like a volunteer tour guide," she explained.

"Oh, that would be fun," said Caitlin.

Derek chuckled. "Caitlin would be a pretty decent docent, don't ya think?"

John gathered them closer on the front porch and began talking. "Some of you may have heard that when we talk about the American Revolution, Patrick Henry has been called the trumpet and George Washington the sword, but does anyone know what Thomas Jefferson was called?" He searched everyone's faces for the answer. Caitlin raised her hand. "Yes?"

"The pen!" she exclaimed proudly. "Since he wrote the Declaration of Independence."

"Very nice, young lady," John said. "But what you'll see as we walk through Monticello, is that another very appropriate name for Jefferson would be 'the professor.' Follow me into the Entrance Hall and see if you can understand where that nickname would come from."

Sam knew Jefferson's house would be like a museum,

since it was so old, but as he stared around the Entrance Hall, it felt like he was in the Smithsonian. All sorts of unusual items filled the wall—huge moose and elk antlers, maps from around the world, animal skins, marble statues, Native American headdresses, bows and arrows, and much more he couldn't immediately identify.

Derek reached a table along the back wall and looked up in surprise. "Wow! A mastodon jawbone!"

Dad cleared his throat. "Let's not touch any of it, though, boys. Okay?"

Derek gave Dad one of his best "I don't know what you're talking about" looks.

John had apparently seen such behavior before and laughed. "This was a waiting room of sorts, designed to entertain the many visitors that came to Monticello. Jefferson had a vast interest in many subjects, and he liked to display his collection for all to see."

"Where did he get it all?" asked Sam, wandering around the room.

"His artifacts came from all over," said John, "but the president's then secretary, Meriwether Lewis, and his friend William Clark gathered some of it. President Jefferson commissioned them to lead an expedition to the new territories acquired from Napoleon and France in 1803."

"The Louisiana Purchase," said Caitlin.

John nodded. "That's right. It nearly doubled the size of the United States, adding a large section west of the Mississippi River stretching from the Gulf of Mexico to

Montana. Their party traveled all the way to the Pacific Ocean on the coast of Oregon and back, encountering amazing things."

Caitlin pointed up at a square box above the front entrance doors. "Is that a clock?"

John walked beneath it. "It's one of Jefferson's most interesting designs."

Sam followed a cable that stretched out from the clock to the edges of the wall. A series of round weights the size of baseballs ran to the floor. "Does this work?" he asked.

"It certainly does," replied John. "The other side of the clock can be seen from the exterior of the house, and those weights you're looking at show the day of the week. They attached to a Chinese gong on the roof, which played each hour and was loud enough to be heard three miles away."

Derek whistled. "We should get one of those for our house, Mom. We could hear you calling us for dinner when we're out in the woods."

"I'm not sure our neighbors would appreciate that," Mom answered.

Sam noticed that days of the week were marked off at different intervals, starting with Sunday at the top of the wall, and ending with Friday along the floor. But something wasn't right. "What happened to Saturday?" He was pretty sure his favorite day of the week was around even in Jefferson's time.

"Even someone like Jefferson had to make accommodations," explained John. "When the clock arrived at Monticello, the mechanism was too tall for the room, so he cut a hole in the floor. Saturday is below us in the basement."

"That's kind of funny," said Derek, deepening his voice. "Uh, Mr. Jefferson, I think we have a problem. It's not gonna fit."

Caitlin pointed to one of the marble statues in the corner. "Is that Alexander Hamilton?"

John nodded. "Yes, it is."

"I thought he and Jefferson didn't like each other?" asked Dad. He'd taken Mom to see the Broadway musical last year when he was in New York for a meeting. The boys hadn't been along, but Sam had heard enough about the story to know that Jefferson and Hamilton were enemies.

John chuckled. "Correct. But notice how their busts sit on opposite sides of the room. Jefferson said the two adversaries would be 'opposed in death as in life.'"

"Geez," said Derek. "He didn't mess around. We should get statues like that of us, Sam."

Dad shook his head. "Or you could just try to get along."

Sam sighed. "Now *that* would be a historic event."

CHAPTER TEN

S am started to lose track of all the unique devices and features as they moved throughout the house. There were parlor doors that opened automatically because of a chain below the floor, a dumbwaiter in the side of the fireplace that delivered wine bottles from the cellar, and a wall alcove that held Jefferson's bed. It was incredible.

"Look," said Caitlin, pointing to the next room. "The library! Now we're getting closer to finding something."

"I thought you said there was a dome?" Derek whispered as they walked through the hall.

"It must be upstairs," said Sam as they entered two connecting rooms where he could see a globe, a telescope, and lots of books and papers. It reminded him of the study in the Wythe House in Colonial Williamsburg, which made sense, since he remembered George Wythe was Jefferson's law professor in college. In that room, they'd found a solar microscope that Wythe had used to project images onto the wall for his students.

"Books were some of Jefferson's most prized possessions," explained John. "In fact, we believe he had the largest personal collection of books in the country. But when the British burned the Library of Congress during the War of 1812—"

"Hang on," said Derek. "Everybody knows that we defeated the British. You know, George Washington and all?"

"Let him finish, Derek," said Dad.

"This was some time later," said John. "After Jefferson had left the presidency. After the fire, Jefferson sold his collection to Congress for 24,000 dollars, which would equal more than fourteen times that amount in today's dollars."

Sam's ears perked up. "His collection?"

"The books, Sam," said Dad. "Pay attention, kids. I'm sorry, John, please continue."

"Sadly, another fire destroyed nearly two-thirds of *that* collection in 1851. Later, when Jefferson was struggling financially near the end of his life, he sold his second collection as well."

"I didn't know that," said Mom.

Sam didn't understand how someone as famous as Thomas Jefferson could be poor. He had been the president, after all. He pointed to an odd-looking object on Jefferson's desk. "What's that?"

"That," said John, "is a polygraph machine."

"Polygraph?" said Caitlin. "Like a lie detector?"

Derek's eyes lit up. "Here, Sam, sit down. Let's see if there's anything you're not scared of."

"Same word," said John, "but different meaning. Jefferson's polygraph was more like a copy machine. He used it to make duplicates of the letters he wrote. It's a reason so much of his writing still exists today."

"That's really smart," said Sam, inspecting how the wooden apparatus moved a second pen that mirrored everything the first pen wrote.

Caitlin raised her hand. "Did Jefferson write a lot of letters to his granddaughters?"

John nodded. "Absolutely. Back then, letters were the only means of communicating. There were no telephones, Internet messages, or texts. The telegraph wasn't even invented until after Jefferson died. But he was quite fond of his grandchildren, many of whom lived here at Monticello in his later years."

"I have a letter from his granddaughters," Caitlin blurted out. "I mean, I saw it at the library. It said they used to play together in the Dome Room. Is that here at Monticello?"

John nodded. "It's up on the third floor—however, we won't be seeing that room today."

"We won't?" Caitlin's face sunk. "Oh, no."

"Why aren't we going there?" asked Sam. That was the reason they'd come to Monticello in the first place.

"I'm afraid that is only on our 'behind the scenes' tour," replied John.

"Maybe we can do that next time," suggested Mom.

Caitlin shook her head. "I guess." She turned to Sam and whispered, "This is terrible."

The tour finished outside on a long terrace overlooking the yard. A small, square building was attached to the terrace like a guesthouse. A sign labeled it as the South Pavilion, Jefferson's newlywed suite.

"Since you seemed interested in Jefferson's books and letters, you should visit the Library of Congress," added John.

Mom looked interested. "I don't think we've made it there yet."

"They have a wonderful exhibit that recreates the original collection Jefferson sold to Congress."

"But I thought the books burned?" asked Sam.

"Just two-thirds of them," said Mom. "Remember?"

"Exactly," said John. "Some are the actual remaining books that Jefferson owned, but they've also located copies of many of the same books that were in his collection. It's quite an undertaking."

"That's pretty cool," said Derek.

"There are still about two hundred and fifty books that the library has been unable to find," John added.

"That's a shame," said Caitlin.

"The library is continuing the search, of course, but it's quite possible they were obscure texts that have been lost to history."

Mom pointed across the lawn, past an oval-shaped fishpond, to a line of people assembling at the pavilion along the side of the yard. "Is that another tour over by the gardens?"

John checked his watch. "Yes, the garden tour should be starting in a few minutes."

"Oh, I'd like to see that," Mom said.

Dad chuckled. "I think that's our cue, kids."

Sam looked around. He didn't want to tour the gardens. They needed to get up to the Dome Room. He turned back toward the corner of the house where another tour group was lined up. His eyes caught a flash of red hair on someone walking into the Entrance Hall. He spun back around and caught his breath.

Derek seemed to notice Sam's expression and said, "We're going to just walk around while you're on the tour, okay? Caitlin will keep us in line. Promise."

"As usual," said Caitlin.

Mom and Dad agreed, and when they were out of earshot, Derek turned around. "What's the matter with you now, Sam? You look like you're about to puke."

Sam glanced back toward the entrance, but the tour line had already entered the house. "She's here!"

"Who?" asked Caitlin.

"Who do you think? The girl with the red hair! I just saw her in the tour line headed into the house. I think she's following us!"

"Why would she be following us?" asked Derek. "I think your imagination is working overtime."

"Either way," said Caitlin, "we have to get to the Dome Room."

"But you heard John," said Sam. "It's closed."

"He didn't say it was closed," Derek answered. "He just said it wasn't part of our tour."

"What's the difference?"

Derek patted Sam's shoulder and smiled. "The difference is you give up too easily. There's always a way in if you want it bad enough. Come on."

CHAPTER ELEVEN

Derek led them swiftly down the passageway that connected the North Wing to the main house. They slipped into the basement, going past the kitchen, wine and beer cellars, and other supply rooms. Sam noticed a clear tube where the weights sank through the floor of the Entrance Hall. Sure enough, there was Saturday from the day-of-the-week clock.

Derek pointed to a narrow staircase around the corner. "There's our way in," he whispered.

"How do you know it goes to the Dome Room?" asked Sam.

"I saw it during our tour," Derek answered. "Two central staircases lead up and down through the house. Believe it or not, I do pay attention to some things."

"What if they see us?" Sam asked.

"Let's just be quick," urged Caitlin. She glanced around to make sure no one was looking and then tiptoed up the steep, narrow steps. They paused behind the corner at the first-floor hallway to let a tour group pass, then scurried up the next flight of stairs, which were even more narrow than those from the basement. There was barely enough room to walk, and Sam had to hold the handrail to keep his balance. He couldn't imagine how Jefferson brought furniture to the upper floors. The second-floor hallway connected several bedrooms and had a balcony overlooking the Entrance Hall. Sam realized that Jefferson must have designed his house to be far bigger than it looked from the outside.

"We need to go one floor higher," said Derek, but Caitlin stopped at an open door.

"Hang on a second. It's *their* room."

"Whose room?" asked Sam.

"The granddaughters. Ellie and Nelly."

"How do you know?"

"I can just tell." She stepped through the doorway, her face all dreamy-eyed. "Look at the ribbons—their clothes and shoes, and look at those flower paintings! I can just tell this is where the sisters would stay. I read that Nelly was very artistic. Maybe these are her drawings." She peered out the window. "Can't you just imagine living here?"

"Yeah, it's amazing," said Derek, "but if you ever want to be allowed to come back, we need to keep moving before someone sees us. We're looking for the Dome Room, remember?"

Caitlin finally relented, and they climbed a final steep

staircase. Down a hallway, light streamed into a wide-angled room with bright yellow walls. An intricate white-paneled dome ceiling rose above them with a circular skylight in the center.

"Wow," said Sam, staring up at the skylight. "It *is* just like the Rotunda at UVA." The sunshine streamed through the glass, casting a round shadow onto the floor.

"John said that Jefferson was inspired by the skylights he saw in France," said Caitlin. "This is one of his signature designs."

"Kind of like one of my signature dance moves," said Derek, twisting his hips and breaking into an awkward spin.

Sam rolled his eyes. "Yeah, just like that."

Caitlin followed the walls of the octagon-shaped room, running her hand along the matching round windows that sank into the walls on every side, like portholes on a ship. "Architecture was one of Jefferson's biggest passions. He loved to tear things down and build them up again to bring them closer to the vision in his head."

"He liked to tinker," said Sam.

Caitlin laughed. "I guess you could say that."

"So what are we looking for?" asked Derek. "I don't see any fairies."

"There weren't *actual* fairies," sighed Caitlin. "That's just what they called their secret place. It was where they liked to hang out and play, like a fort. Maybe it's hidden in the wall."

Two brown wooden doors were on the far wall. "Does this lead to the next bedroom?" asked Sam, pulling one side open. He caught his breath. "Whoa, it's like a secret room."

Caitlin ran over. "You found it! The Cuddy."

Sam stuck his head into the space and looked around. It was no bigger than the walk-in closet in his parents' bedroom, but it looked more like part of the attic. The floor sunk down three feet from the floor of the Dome Room. Inside was a short table, a small sofa, and a sitting chair that were all covered with white sheets. It *did* seem like a hidden playhouse. Light poured through a small, arched half-window directly across from the doors. He could see the lawn and gardens in the back of the house, and he hoped Mom and Dad didn't walk by and look up.

"Let me through, Sam." Derek pushed past and dropped down to the floor. "We can't take all day."

"He's right," said Caitlin. "We have to hurry before someone comes in." She climbed down and began searching the brick walls beside the doorway and the wooden rafters in the ceiling.

"We'll be in big trouble if they find us back here."

"Just shut up and search, Sam," said Derek.

Caitlin crouched along the brickwork below the doorway. "The letter said they used a loose brick to hide things."

"But that was two hundred years ago. What if they've remodeled it or cemented the brick into the wall?" Sam leaned into the corners, inspecting the hidden spaces. He searched for loose bricks, but each one he tugged was rock solid. It felt like he was touching the bones of Jefferson's house. He stepped further into the rafters, moving carefully onto the beams that held the ceiling of the room below.

He remembered the time when Dad had fallen through the attic of their old house up north. He'd been working to install a ceiling fan, but his foot missed a joist and he fell straight through the ceiling. Thankfully, he landed on Derek's bed and his only injury was to his pride. Still, it made a huge mess, and they'd had to pay a contractor to fix the ceiling. Sam couldn't imagine the consequences of falling through the ceiling of Thomas Jefferson's house. It would be unforgivable.

Sam turned back toward the door, but his face brushed through a wide spider web that stretched across the beams. As he waved his hand to get the sticky substance off, his eyes focused on a dark spot on the nearest rafter. A huge, black spider sat motionless, like it was waiting for Sam to become fully entangled in its web before moving in for the attack. Sam jerked away from the spider, but he moved too quickly and his foot slipped off the joist. He lost his balance and tumbled toward the plaster ceiling.

Derek's hand shot out and caught Sam's arm, softening his fall, and pulling him back onto the floorboards.

"Smooth, Sam."

"Thanks," he answered sheepishly. That was a close one.

Before he could stand up, Sam noticed a gap between the floorboards and the brick. His outstretched arm just fit into the open space, and he ran his fingers over the rough brick surface. A chunk of mortar fell loose from his touch. A brick shifted.

"Uh, I think I found a loose one," he called back up.

"A brick?" asked Caitlin, moving behind him.

"Yeah." Sam reached further in, straining against the wood. He slid the brick back, using his fingers like tongs. An opening developed where the brick had rested. He stretched even further, expecting his hand to hit another brick or board, but it kept going.

"There's a space in here," he called.

He felt something soft, like paper. He caught his breath and tightened his fingers around the edge.

"Another letter?" whispered Caitlin.

"Maybe," Sam grunted, straining to squeeze tighter. "I almost have it."

Whatever was there, he didn't want to rip it. He carefully pulled back his hand, and the paper came loose.

"Got it!" he called back. "Pull me up."

Derek and Caitlin tugged on Sam's shoulder until he was sitting securely back in the room.

"Oh my gosh," said Caitlin, staring at the paper in his hand. It was yellowed and crinkled and had rolled up with age.

Sam began to pull gently at the edge, but it started to crumble.

"Wait," cried Caitlin. "We have to be careful. We can't lose it now."

She placed the paper on the floor and gradually flattened the page. The writing was faded, but mostly legible. It was in the same old-style cursive as the journal and the other letter they'd found. There seemed to be a drawing below the words.

"Just a sec," said Caitlin, pulling out her phone. "Let me take a picture before it completely falls apart." She tapped to take a photo, but then, as she leaned closer to read the writing, voices boomed from the room above them. At first Sam thought someone was right outside the door, but he realized the domed ceiling had amplified the sound. Someone was coming up the stairwell.

"Quick, hide!" Derek reached up and pulled the Dome Room door closed.

Sam quickly rolled the paper back up and stuck it in his pocket. Caitlin squeezed to the side of the brick cutout in the wall to the left of the door, while Derek found a similar space to the right. There wasn't enough room for Sam to join either of them, so he crouched behind the sofa below the window. He felt exposed, but there was no other place to hide. Hopefully, whoever was coming wouldn't look closely, or they'd see him.

"Young lady," a woman's voice called urgently. "Just a minute, please. As I explained, this area is not part of the tour."

Sam peered around the side of the sofa as footsteps banged across the wooden floor of the Dome Room. He could barely see the door, but he held still, the remains of a cobweb still hanging from his ear. The letter from the granddaughters had said nothing about spiders, and he hoped the wasps and bees they'd mentioned were long gone.

"Ma'am, you really can't come up here," the woman called again.

"I'll only be a minute," a second, younger-sounding female voice answered.

Sam didn't recognize the voice, but somehow he knew who it was. He'd seen the flash of red hair in the tour line. It had to be her. She seemed to be everywhere they'd gone. But why would she be in the Dome Room? Was she following them, or had another entry in the journal mentioned the treasure?

"What's through here?" the younger voice asked, her footsteps stopping just outside the door.

"Why, that's the Cuddy space, nothing but a closet," replied the first woman. "Despite the unique appearance of this room, it was used mostly only as storage and as an extra playroom for the grandchildren. But young lady, I really must ask that you leave now, before I call security."

The Cuddy door cracked open. Sam pushed lower to the floor. He saw a shoe, then a leg, stretch through the doorway. She was coming. Sam slid forward, trying to keep the sofa between him and the girl. A lock of long red hair fell into his view. He saw her face, just like in the library. He held his breath as their eyes locked, seemingly for minutes. She'd seen him.

But then she turned. She pulled her leg back up to the Dome Room. What was she doing? He was sure that she'd seen him. Why was she leaving?

The squawk of a radio followed by a man's voice came from the next room. "Is there a problem, ma'am?"

"I tried to explain that this room was not a part of the tour, but this young lady just won't listen," the exasperated older woman said. For once, Sam was glad to hear that security had arrived.

"Sorry, I was just leaving," the red-haired girl answered. The door to the Cuddy closed. Footsteps sounded across the Dome Room floor and down the stairway.

Sam finally exhaled. He prayed the Cuddy doors hadn't locked, or they'd be trapped.

"That was close," said Caitlin, standing from her hiding place. "I thought she was going to see you."

"She did."

"What?"

"She did," Sam repeated. "She looked right at me."

"But she didn't say anything?" asked Derek.

Sam shook his head.

"Where's the paper?" asked Caitlin. "I'm dying to know what it says."

Sam had almost forgotten about the paper. He reached into his pocket and pulled out the curled paper, but it had cracked even more, and as he grasped it, the yellow paper disintegrated in his hands.

"Sam!" cried Derek. "What did you do?"

"I didn't do anything. It was old."

"Unbelievable," Derek moaned.

"Sorry," said Sam. "I had to hide fast."

Caitlin held up her phone. "It's okay. I took a picture, remember?"

"Thanks," said Sam, feeling better. He looked out the window at the back lawn. He saw the girl walking away from the house, waving her arms at the security man.

"Still think it wasn't the same redheaded girl?" Sam asked, pointing at the scene.

"She's up to something," said Caitlin.

"But what?" asked Sam.

Derek climbed up to the Dome Room. "I don't know, but we need to sneak out of here before security comes back."

"What about the picture?" asked Caitlin.

"We can inspect it outside," said Derek. "Come on."

CHAPTER TWELVE

They snuck back down the central staircase without seeing anyone, but a woman eyed them suspiciously when they reached the basement. "Where are you three headed?" she asked.

"Sorry," said Sam, recognizing the voice of the woman who'd called security up in the Dome Room. "We're trying to find the restrooms."

She raised an eyebrow but pointed down the basement corridor. "They're around the side next to the gift shop."

"Thanks," said Caitlin, laughing as they hurried through a wooden door. "You always use that excuse, Sam."

He grinned. "It always works."

They entered a long corridor that was set into the ground with half-circle windows up near the ceiling beams by their heads. Around the corner, they passed a wide, circular wall capped by a wooden covering. Sam pointed to iron bars that blocked the opening to a dark space. "What's that?"

"I hope that's not where they threw runaway slaves," said Derek.

Caitlin shook her head and pointed to the sign. "It's the icehouse. Washington had one at Mount Vernon too, remember? He brought blocks of ice up from the river and stored them here throughout the year."

"It would still make a good jail," said Derek. He tugged on the bars, but they were locked by a metal latch.

"Didn't the ice melt?" Sam tried to remember how that worked, but it didn't seem to make sense. "It's hot all summer long, even up here on the mountain." He crouched down and shaded his eyes to see through the bars into the dark hole. "Oh... wow, that's big." The cylinder-shaped bricked space was a dozen feet across and the same distance below them.

"It's set into the ground to keep cool."

"I'll ask if you can hang out down there for a while, Derek," said Sam. "You know, since you think you're so cool already."

Derek took a threatening step toward him. "How about I throw you over the edge of the mountain here, and you can see how long it takes to roll to Charlottesville?"

"Stop it, you two," said Caitlin. "We need to look at the message." She pulled up the picture on her phone.

"It's another short note and what looks like a map." They all leaned in to read.

Dearest Ellen, this is the best drawing I could muster from the details told to me on one of our long trips to Poplar Forest. I heard that the collection had been hidden in a space behind the old fireplace, but that has been long since covered, and I have no certainty. Do you remember the basement kitchen where James made the most extraordinary French meals? What I wouldn't give to someday be the one who could find it. Affectionately yours, C.R.

Below the words was a rough sketch showing a small compartment behind an area that could be a fireplace.

"Poplar Forest," said Sam. "That was the vacation home that we read about in the journal, right?"

"It has to be," said Caitlin.

"What's a poplar?" asked Derek.

"A kind of tree, I think," Caitlin answered. "But that's also the name of the house. They talk about the kitchen, and James, who I think might be James Hemings, another one of the enslaved workers."

"Is he related to Sally?" asked Sam.

"I would think so. Probably the same family."

"Let me see that picture again," said Derek. Caitlin handed him her phone, and he zoomed in on the image of the drawing beneath the letter. "I guess that could be a drawing of a kitchen," he said. "But do you think it's still there?"

"The treasure?" asked Sam.

"No, the kitchen. I mean, it's been two hundred years. If they hid something behind the fireplace, what's the chance that it hasn't been destroyed?"

"I don't know," Caitlin admitted, shaking her head.

Sam's phone buzzed in his pocket. "It's Mom. They're already heading to the visitor center. She says we should start walking down to meet them."

"We can walk and talk," said Caitlin. "We need to keep following these clues. The granddaughters clearly want us to find this collection."

Sam shook his head. "They want us to find it, huh?"

"That's right. It's like the universe sent it our way." Caitlin twirled a strand of her hair as they walked. "It's like fate."

"Uh-huh," said Sam. "Fate or no fate, we still don't even know what's in this collection, or if it still exists at all."

"I think it's something awesome," said Derek.

Caitlin smiled wide. "Thank you."

"And how would you know that, genius?" Sam hated how his brother acted so confident about everything, even when he didn't have a clue what he was talking about.

"Well, first off, I'm incredibly lucky, so there's a good chance I've stumbled onto something important again."

"*We* stumbled upon it, Derek. You weren't anywhere near the journal."

"Second," Derek added, ignoring Sam's argument, "there was no reason for the sisters to write about it if it wasn't important."

Caitlin nodded. "He's right. If it wasn't valuable, they wouldn't have spoken of it."

That did make sense. "Okay, but even if that's true, what do we do next?"

Caitlin stared at him like it was obvious. "Just like Nelly suggested, we have to get to Poplar Forest and see if we can find this fireplace in the kitchen."

Sam let Derek and Caitlin walk ahead to jabber on about the clues. Caitlin was being almost as annoying as Derek. He stopped next to a structure on Mulberry Row and stared at the view from the mountain. He wondered again how it must have felt to live at this magnificent plantation when it was still Jefferson's home.

"Sam, are you coming or what?" Derek called.

"Yeah." Sam glanced back at the Hemings' cabin on Mulberry Row. Like a lot of the historic places they'd visited, a lot depended on who you were. Just like Washington's Mount Vernon, the plantation couldn't have operated without the dozens of enslaved workers who labored in the fields, grounds, and inside the house. It had probably been a whole different experience from their perspective.

Sam caught up with Derek and Caitlin further down the hill as they approached a tall, black metal fence that surrounded a small cemetery. It looked different from George Washington's brick tomb and above-ground stone casket at Mount Vernon. This one looked more like a regular cemetery, like where George Wythe was buried at St. John's Church. There was a gold-painted "TJ" emblem emblazoned with a fancy symbol on the gates.

Sam peeked through the metal bars. Dozens of graves filled the grassy area. "Where's Jefferson?"

"I think there are several Jeffersons in there," said Caitlin. "But that one looks important." She pointed to a medium-sized obelisk behind another gate to their right. They walked over and stood reverently for a moment. There was something impressive about the burial place of a former president.

"That's weird," said Caitlin, quietly.

"What?" asked Sam.

"The inscription. Notice anything missing?"

Sam hadn't read past the name. He looked more carefully now.

"HERE WAS BURIED
THOMAS JEFFERSON
AUTHOR OF THE
DECLARATION
OF
AMERICAN INDEPENDENCE
OF THE
STATUTE OF VIRGINIA
FOR

RELIGEOUS FREEDOM
AND FATHER OF THE
UNIVERSITY OF VIRGINIA."

That all sounded correct. But then it hit him. "It doesn't say he was president."

"Maybe it was a typo," said Derek. "That happens a lot."

"It wasn't a typo, Derek."

"He must have chosen not to mention it," said Caitlin. "Maybe he considered the other three things more important."

"That's hard to believe," said Derek.

Sam remembered something John had said on their tour, that Jefferson called the presidency "a daily loss of friends." "Maybe he just didn't like it."

"I guess," said Derek. "But if I was president, I'd have that put at the top of the list."

"Thankfully for all of us, you're not," said Sam.

"Quite an interesting man, wasn't he?" The familiar voice came from around the corner of the fence. Sam looked up and caught his breath. It was her.

The red-haired girl walked toward them and stopped in front of Jefferson's grave marker. "He was a giant in history, yet full of contradictions."

Derek looked up in surprise. "That's what I said!"

Sam took in the girl, finally able to see her up close and for more than a quick second. Caitlin was right—she was too young to be a doctor, but she could be a college student. She seemed around the same age as his cousin Meghan. Her long red hair was distinctive, and he thought he saw the glimmer of a gold nose ring in the light.

Sam crossed his arms. "Are you following us?"

She smiled. "I couldn't help but notice that we were both admiring Jefferson's house on the same day. Quite the coincidence, isn't it?"

"I doubt that," said Caitlin.

The girl ignored Caitlin's comment and extended her hand. "My name's Aubrey."

Sam and Caitlin stood where they were, but Derek stepped up and shook her hand. Sam glanced at Caitlin, and if looks could kill, then she'd be wanted for murder for sure.

"I always love meeting people with common interests," Aubrey said.

"What interest is that?" Caitlin said finally. "Crime? Sorry, we have no interest in that."

Aubrey frowned. "No... a love of history."

"Love?" scoffed Caitlin. "You're just a thief."

"We know you stole the journal from the bookstore," said Sam. "That was ours."

Aubrey held up her hands. "I'm not a thief. I'm just..." She paused, searching for the right word. "Interested."

Caitlin's face was red. "Are you saying you didn't steal the journal from my mom's bookstore? We saw the security tape. It was you."

"Okay, I may have made a mistake there. I'm sorry. I don't know what I was thinking. Haven't you ever been in a situation where you were just overwhelmed by the moment and did something stupid?"

Derek quickly nodded. "All the time!"

Sam motioned for his brother to shut his mouth, but he realized that would be like putting toothpaste back in the tube.

"I'll tell you what." Aubrey reached into the pack slung over her shoulder. She pulled out the old journal and held it out to Caitlin. "No hard feelings?"

Sam raised his eyebrows. He hadn't seen that coming.

Caitlin tentatively stepped forward. "Thanks…," she said softly, taking the journal.

"Okay, I'm confused," said Derek. "If you're not following us, and you don't want to keep the journal, what are you doing here?"

That was a good question. This whole thing didn't make any sense. Sam started to squirm. "Our parents are expecting us down at the visitor center."

Aubrey raised her hand again. "Hear me out for two minutes. Despite our awkward introduction, I love to collect history. My dad got me into it when I was about your age, and it's stuck ever since. I'm a first year at UVA. Now, it's what I do for fun. We don't know each other, but after seeing you three at the Special Collections Library and now again here at Monticello, I have to guess that you're like me."

Derek flashed a cocky grin. "We've been known to track down some important history now and then."

Sam glared again at his brother.

"What?" said Derek. "Maybe she's heard of us."

"Let's acknowledge the elephant in the room," said Aubrey. "We both know that journal is pointing to a hidden treasure."

Caitlin shook her head. "We don't know what you're talking about."

"Sure," replied Aubrey, staring at Caitlin. "If you read those letters between the sisters, you know that this is something special. You must already be looking for it. And just guessing here, but I don't think any of you are old enough to drive. Am I right?"

"Well…" Derek stuttered. "I'll get my driver's permit in a couple… years."

Aubrey chuckled. "Right, so you're here with your parents, which means you're probably having a hard time doing everything you need to do. I could help you with that."

Sam narrowed his eyes. "What exactly are you proposing?"

Aubrey's grin was just like Derek's when he was trying to convince their parents of something. "Why don't we work together? You'd be surprised what I could add to the mix." She reached back in her bag and pulled out a note card and a pen. She scribbled something and handed it to Caitlin. "Here's my number. Think about it, okay?"

"We have to go," said Caitlin, grabbing Sam's arm.

"Your parents are waiting for us." They stepped down the path to the visitor center, and when the three of them were out of sight, they broke into a jog.

"Hang on a second, will ya?" called Sam when they reached the life-sized bronze statue of Thomas Jefferson at the bottom of the trail. His stomach was in knots.

"What's the matter?" asked Caitlin.

His jaw dropped. "What's the matter? Are you serious?"

"Stop yelling," said Derek. "You're going to draw attention."

"I'll tell you what's the matter," Sam said again, trying to keep his voice down. "This is crazy. She has to be up to something. First she steals the journal, and now she wants to be our best friend? Something's not right."

"She gave it back, didn't she?" said Derek. "Maybe she had a change of heart."

"Or she read the journal and got everything she needed from it," said Caitlin.

"Caitlin's right," said Derek. "Think about it for a second. Why do you think she approached us?"

"I don't know," said Sam. "Maybe because she's psycho?"

"You've watched too many movies, Sam," Derek said. "If she didn't need us, she would have just kept looking on her own. She could have busted us in the Cuddy, but she didn't say anything. That has to count for something."

CHAPTER THIRTEEN

The ride back home to Richmond was fairly quiet. Caitlin read from her phone most of the way, but Sam couldn't stop thinking about Aubrey's offer.

"You guys all right back there?" Dad called from the front. "I've never seen you three so quiet."

"I'm just doing some reading on Thomas Jefferson," answered Caitlin. "It's hard not to be inspired after seeing all that history."

"Yeah," Derek added. "What she said."

"Did you guys remember that Dad and I have a dinner tonight for Dad's work?" asked Mom.

"Where are you going again?" asked Sam.

"Actually, it's at the Jefferson Hotel," said Dad.

Caitlin laughed. "That's appropriate."

"You know, I hadn't even thought about that until now," said Mom. "We had these plans long before you all asked to go to Charlottesville."

Sam thought back to the time they'd spent a weekend at the historic hotel for Mom's friend Anita's wedding. The Jefferson was amazing, but it wasn't like Monticello. Thomas Jefferson didn't actually live there; they only named it after him. Lewis Ginter had built the hotel, and bizarrely, it had once had alligators in the lobby fountains. Things had got a little out of hand that weekend, and Sam was in no hurry to go back.

"Can we come along?" asked Derek.

"Not this time. Sorry, guys," said Dad.

Mom turned around to look at them from her seat. "But, Caitlin, if you'd like to stay for a while, I'll order a pizza and the boys will probably watch a movie. We can take you home when we get back, or your parents can come get you whenever you'd like."

Caitlin glanced at Sam to see what he thought. He could tell from the smile on her face she wanted to do it, so he nodded.

"Sure," said Caitlin. "That sounds fun. Thanks!"

"There's a strong chance of thunderstorms tonight," said Dad, "so make sure you keep the windows shut. And watch that back window in my office. We had a leak the last time it rained hard."

"I think we can handle it, Dad," said Derek.

* * *

THE PIZZA WAS STILL PIPING hot when Mom carried the box out to the back deck. The sky was growing darker, but so far the rain had held off.

"We'll be home by ten," said Mom, "but call if you have any problems."

"Got it, Mom," said Derek. "It's not like we're in kindergarten anymore." He glanced at Sam and chuckled. "Well, most of us, at least."

Sam rolled his eyes. "I think we'll be fine."

"See you, Mrs. Jackson," said Caitlin. "Thanks for the pizza." She waited for Sam's parents' car to pull down the driveway, and then she turned serious. "I did a lot of reading in the car. We have to figure this out."

"I thought we were watching a movie," said Derek. "The new Avengers movie is on Netflix this month."

"Hmm," said Caitlin. "I was hoping we could talk more about the clues."

Derek sighed. "Or we could do that."

"And we have to discuss Aubrey," said Caitlin.

Sam groaned. He didn't like how they'd run into her at Jefferson's grave, and he didn't like the idea of working with some stranger just because she'd asked. They'd always worked alone, and from his experience, most people had ulterior motives.

A gust of wind blew Sam's napkin across the table and off the deck. The heavy clouds were further darkening the evening sky. "Storm's coming."

"We'd better get going on that movie then," said Derek, standing up.

"Okay," relented Caitlin, "but afterward, we're researching the letter. Don't you care about finding the collection?"

"Sure," said Derek, rubbing his hands together. "But I also want to see something being blown up."

"You're such a boy," Caitlin muttered.

"I'll take that as a compliment," said Derek as he turned out the lights. Sam pulled up the movie listings on the television, but Derek tried to grab the remote. "Let me do it, Sam. You always hit the wrong buttons."

"I do not." He clicked on the movie list, but suddenly the monitor went dark.

Derek moaned. "See what I mean?"

Sam pressed the power button on the remote again, but nothing happened. "I didn't do anything." He leaned around the corner and saw the lights were also off in the kitchen.

"I think the storm knocked out the power," said Caitlin.

"Or Sam blew out the grid by pushing the wrong button."

"Like that's even possible," Sam sneered.

Derek reached up and flicked the light switch again, but nothing happened. "Well, that stinks. What are we supposed to do now?"

Caitlin stood and opened the sliding door to the deck. "Listen to that wind blowing through the trees. Let's go back out here until it starts raining."

"She wants to listen to the wind?" said Derek. "What's wrong with that girlfriend of yours, Sam?"

Sam slugged him in the shoulder. "Just because Mom and Dad aren't here doesn't mean you have to go back to being a jerk."

Derek grabbed a flashlight, and they pulled the chairs into a half-circle. The tops of the trees danced in the wind like ships bobbing up and down in giant ocean swells.

"Okay, you got your wish. We're talking. What did you find out in your research?" Derek shined the flashlight on Caitlin's face like a spotlight.

She held her arm up over her face. "Ow, not in my eyes, Derek."

"Sorry." He handed her the flashlight. "Hold it under your chin while you talk. It's spookier."

"Fine." Caitlin held the light below her face, casting creepy shadows. "Better?"

"Perfect."

"So, I read more about the different people named Hemings. They were from the same family. In fact, Sally was one of several children Thomas Jefferson inherited through his wife Martha's family."

"Inherited?" asked Sam. "How can you inherit a person?"

"Exactly. But they were slaves and could be passed along to your heirs just like property."

It was hard for Sam to even picture how that could work, or how someone like Jefferson could allow it. "Why didn't he free them?"

"I'm not sure," said Caitlin. "He said he wanted to, but he never really fought to end slavery. He said that slavery in America was like holding a wolf by the ears—you didn't like it, but you couldn't let go."

"What the heck does that mean?" asked Derek.

"I guess it means he was conflicted," answered Caitlin. "Just like with the Hemings family. Sally traveled to Paris with Jefferson when he was ambassador, along with her brother James, who was trained to be a French chef. Another brother, Martin, was Jefferson's butler."

"That's who hid the valuables," said Sam. "He was a Heming too?"

Caitlin nodded in the light.

"Speaking of the valuables," said Derek. "You really think some treasure could still be there after all this time?"

Caitlin shrugged. "The letter was still in the Cuddy. And based on that, I think we need to find the kitchen in Poplar Forest."

"Is that near Richmond?" asked Derek.

"No. That's the problem," said Caitlin. "It's about two hours from here, just outside Lynchburg."

"I don't know if our parents will want to drive us all to another place after they just took us to Charlottesville," said Sam. "At least, not without a lot more explanation."

"What about Aubrey?" asked Derek.

"What about her?" said Caitlin.

"You heard her," said Derek. "She practically offered to be our chauffeur. She could drive us to Poplar Forest."

"We don't even know her," said Sam.

"I'm still deciding what I think about her," Caitlin added. "I was reading more of the journal in the car. Ellie and Nelly feel like my own sisters. I really want to know what they're talking about. Maybe it really was just a coincidence that Aubrey ended up at the same place as us again. She could be helpful."

"That's one heck of a coincidence," said Sam.

"We'll never know if we don't go there," said Derek, as a ringing sounded inside the house.

"Is that your phone?" asked Caitlin.

Sam patted his phone in his pocket. "Not mine." And it certainly wasn't Derek's ringtone.

"It sounds like the landline," said Derek. Mom insisted on keeping a corded phone in the house that she called the "landline" in case of emergencies or if their cell phones died.

"I thought the power was out?" said Sam.

"It must still work," said Caitlin.

Sam nodded to the doorway. "Are you going to answer it?"

Derek shook his head. "You're closer."

"Yeah, by like six inches—" Sam started to object but stopped himself. Sometimes it just wasn't worth it.

He went inside to the old phone plugged on the kitchen wall. The only people that ever called on that number were telemarketers and politicians, but maybe it was the power company. He picked up the clunky receiver. "Hello?"

There was static on the line. It must be a bad connection because of the storm.

"*Hello?*" he said again.

He was about to hang up when a woman's voice came across the line.

"I have a collect call from Hollow's Ridge Prison for Sam or Derek. Do you accept the charges?"

CHAPTER FOURTEEN

S am stood frozen, the phone receiver still pushed against his ear. A flash of lightning filled the room with brightness, and an almost immediate boom of thunder brought Derek and Caitlin scrambling in from the deck.

"Sir," the voice said again through the phone. "Do you accept the charges?"

"Uh, hang on," Sam muttered, passing Derek the phone. "It's for you."

"Me? Is it Aubrey? Why's she calling on this line?" He took the receiver, smiling like whoever was on the other end could see him. "Talk to me." His eyes opened wide at the reply. "Sure!" he said.

"Who is it?" whispered Caitlin.

Sam felt his heart racing. "Someone from prison."

"Prison?"

"That's what they said. But they're trying to collect a call or something."

"Collect a call?" Caitlin frowned. "You mean a *collect call?*"

"Maybe," said Sam. "What is that?"

"I think it's when the person receiving the call has to pay for it."

"Pay for it?" That didn't make sense either. "Why would you have to pay for a phone call?"

"It must be from a pay phone," said Caitlin.

"A what?"

Caitlin shook her head. "It doesn't matter. Who's calling you from prison?"

"How should I know?" said Sam. "That's why I gave it to him."

Derek was still listening quietly to whoever was talking on the other end of the line.

"Who is it?" whispered Caitlin, but Derek waved her off.

"Uh-huh," he said. "Right… no way…"

It went on like that for a minute or two until Derek finally finished. "Okay, thanks, Ben. We really appreciate it. Good luck in there… uh-huh. Bye." He set the receiver back in its cradle, then stared at them, his eyes wide.

"Well?" asked Sam.

"Well, what?"

"Who was on the phone?" asked Caitlin. "Who's calling you from prison?"

Derek motioned to the couch. "I think you should sit down."

"Okay…," said Sam, moving next to Caitlin on the couch. "Now spill it."

"Well, it all started a few months ago."

"A few months ago?" asked Sam.

Derek nodded. "You see, I got this letter, from a female inmate. She was kind of obsessed with me. Some people might call it stalking, but I don't know, I think she's just lonely and—"

Sam punched Derek's shoulder hard. "Shut up! Will you be serious?" Talking to Derek was like banging your head against a brick wall.

"Derek! Who called?" said Caitlin.

Derek held up his hand. "Okay, sorry, bad timing." He turned serious. "But you're not going to like what Ben had to say."

"Who's Ben?" asked Caitlin.

"He used to be in the Ghosts, with Mad Dog."

"The biker gang?" said Caitlin.

Derek nodded. "But he got pinched."

"Pinched?"

"Put in prison, Sam." Derek sighed. "Come on. Keep up, will you?"

"Why is he in prison?" asked Caitlin.

"No idea. But that's not important." Derek stood and paced the room. "This is the part you're not going to like. I don't like it either. It's kind of bad. Actually, it's terrible. It's about… Jerry."

Sam's stomach sank like he'd swallowed a rock.

"What?" gasped Caitlin.

"What about him?" Sam pictured the man's face in his mind. Shortly after they'd moved to Virginia, they'd all stumbled into Jerry's plot to find a hidden piece of history. He'd chased them all the way from St. John's Church in Richmond to the Wythe House in Colonial Williamsburg. He was not happy when they foiled his plans and he got hauled away by the cops. It was only by the skin of their teeth that they'd gotten away. Sam had been having bad dreams about the man for months.

Derek bit his lip. "So Ben and Jerry were both in prison at Hollow's Ridge. And Ben heard Jerry talking about a plan to get revenge on some kids."

"Oh, no…," said Caitlin.

Sam thought he might hurl. "But Jerry's still locked up, right?" He didn't like hearing that Jerry was talking about getting back at them, but as long as he was behind bars, it seemed like they'd be safe.

"Derek?" said Caitlin, when he didn't answer right away.

"He was. But apparently they released him this morning. That's why Ben was calling us. The landline must be listed in the phone book. Like I said, he used to be in the Ghosts and had heard the guys talking about us and how we were friends with Mad Dog. He put two and two together and wanted to warn us to be careful."

"Careful?" said Sam, starting to sweat. "Of what? Is he coming after us?"

"I don't know," said Derek.

Sam shook his head. "This is beyond bad. This is terrible."

Another clap of thunder shook the house.

Sam leaped from the couch and stood by the window. "He could be out there right now. He's probably the one who cut the power lines!" He peered out into the darkness. Did the rest of the street have power? He couldn't see through the trees to tell if Mr. Haskins' lights were on or not.

"No one cut the power lines," said Derek. "It's just the storm."

"I don't care what you say. I'm telling Mom and Dad."

"I think I'm with Sam this time," said Caitlin.

"Yeah." Derek nodded. "I guess you're right."

Headlights flashed across the cul-de-sac.

"Who's that?" shrieked Sam, sinking to the floor. He peeked over the windowsill and squinted to see through the rain. It was too early for Mom and Dad. Was it Jerry? Did he know where they lived?

Caitlin's phone buzzed and she let out a long breath. "It's just my dad. He's at the end of the driveway to pick me up. Are you guys going to be okay? Do you want me to ask him to come in?"

Derek shook his head. "Nah, we're okay."

She glanced at Sam, who was still hiding below the window. "You sure?"

Sam stood and tried to pull himself together. "Yeah,

our parents will be home soon, and we'll tell them about everything." He walked over and opened the front door for Caitlin. "See ya."

Caitlin squealed as she jumped from the porch, using her arm to shield her face from the rain until she hopped into her dad's truck. Sam waved to Mr. Murphy and then closed the door before the rain blew in. Derek passed him at the base of the foyer staircase. He shined the flashlight up the steps to the dark upstairs hallway.

"Where are you going?" asked Sam.

"I'm gonna take a shower."

"Now?"

Derek shrugged. "There's no TV or Wi-Fi with the power out. I'm bored."

"But what about the phone call? What about Jerry?" Sam knew he might get overly nervous sometimes, but some things needed to be taken seriously. Things like receiving a warning call from prison.

"There's nothing we can do about it now, Sam. We'll tell Mom and Dad when they get home. In the meantime, I'm taking a shower."

"Whatever," Sam muttered. Now that his older brother was a teenager, Mom was always bugging him to bathe, but as usual, he had terrible timing. Sam took the only candle he could find, the pumpkin-scented one from the bathroom, and set it on the kitchen counter. He lit it, giving the room an eerie glow. Shadows flickered across the walls and ceiling from the flame.

Ever since they'd seen Aubrey in the reading room,

he'd sensed that this whole situation with the journal was trouble. Now with Jerry on the loose, it felt like a lion was prowling in the darkness around their house, waiting for his opportunity to burst in and devour them.

Sam looked across the kitchen, suddenly feeling hungry. If Derek could take a shower, then he could get a snack. The refrigerator sat dark and oddly silent without the light or motor running. He quickly poured a glass of milk, replacing the carton and shutting the door to keep the cold air from escaping.

He dunked a couple of chocolate-chip cookies in the milk and walked to the sliding back door. He set his glass down on the counter and flicked on the porch light out of habit. Of course, it didn't work. He peered at the dark outline of the woods. The rain had slowed, but the trees still danced wildly in the wind.

Something caught his eye.

A shadow was drifting across the backyard. It was the figure of a man. Sam jerked away from the glass, pulling the curtain across the door. He pressed against the wall, his heart pounding. Was it Jerry? Who else would be walking across the backyard in the middle of a thunderstorm?

He turned, intending to find Derek, but his elbow knocked into his drinking glass, sending milk across the counter and onto the floor like a waterfall. He grabbed the glass before it fell off the counter and shattered, but milk was everywhere. He stopped and slid back against the wall. He had to think. Maybe he'd just imagined seeing someone. Derek would never let him hear the end of it if he sounded the alarm and no one was there. He had to be sure.

Sam tiptoed back to the door, trying not to think about the sticky milk under his feet. The figure in the backyard was more important. He took a deep breath, pulled the curtain back a sliver, and peered into the darkness. The yard seemed empty. Maybe it had just been his imagination.

Then a dark figure filled the doorway.

CHAPTER FIFTEEN

S am screamed at the figure on the other side of the glass. He lurched from the door, but slipped on the spilled milk. He fell to the floor, landing halfway under the kitchen table.

"Derek!" he cried.

The door handle rattled as someone turned the latch. They were trying to get in the house!

"Derek!" he screamed again, sliding further under the table, just as the sound of jangling keys and the door opening came from the foyer.

"Boys?" Footsteps came down the hallway. "Why are all the lights off?"

"Dad!" Thank goodness.

"Sam? Where are you?"

He crawled from his hiding spot just as his parents walked into the shadowy kitchen.

"Candles?" Mom flicked the light switch. "Is the power out?"

Dad raised an eyebrow. "Playing hide-and-seek?"

"Shh! There's someone out there."

"Out where?" asked Mom.

"On the deck! I saw him looking through the glass." Sam didn't want to launch right into the news about Jerry. "I think it's a burglar."

"A burglar?" asked Dad. "In the middle of the storm?"

Mom looked down at the floor. "Is that milk?"

Dad opened the sliding door just as a loud crash sounded on the deck. It was followed by a moan and a ranting voice. "Doggone rotten no good monkey-livered—"

"Jonas? Is that you?" Dad stepped out on the deck, wind blowing into the kitchen.

Sam let out a deep breath when he heard Mr. Haskins' voice.

"Confounded recycling bin!"

"Are you all right?" asked Dad. "What are you doing out here in the storm?"

A very good question, thought Sam.

"I'm sorry. Didn't mean to disturb y'all." Mr. Haskins' shadow came back into view through the doorway. "I thought I'd left my extension cord over here last week. The power's out, and I wanted to get my generator up and running before everything in my fridge goes bad. Believe it or not, I just bought a dozen pork chops." He brushed his wet hands over his pant legs. "Sorry to be a bother."

"Oh… it's no problem," said Dad. "We just got home." He pushed the sliding glass door wider and gestured for him to come inside. "Come on in and sit with Sam. I think I put that extension cord in the garage."

"Let me get you a towel," said Mom, as the old man limped through the door and eased himself into one of the kitchen chairs. She moved the candle to the center of the table.

"Thank you kindly. I was trying to avoid falling down and breaking my bones, but I seem to have nearly done that anyway." Mr. Haskins glanced over at Sam. "I didn't scare you out there, did I?"

"No," Sam lied. "Just surprised, that's all." They sat across the table for a few seconds in silence, trying not to stare at each other through the flickering light. Sam felt like one of them was about to draw their revolver, like in an old Western.

"Got any more milk?"

"What?"

"Got any milk, I say." Mr. Haskins banged his palm on the table. "You asleep or something?"

Sam gave the old man a crooked stare, but stood and walked to the cupboard for another glass.

"What's all the yelling?" said Derek, entering the kitchen with only a towel wrapped around his waist.

"Whoa, I didn't know we were having a party. Hey, Mr. Haskins!"

"You goin' streakin'?"

Derek laughed. "Quite a storm, huh?"

"Nah," said Mr. Haskins, reaching down to rub his shin. "This is nothin'. Back in '03, Isabelle rolled through and knocked the power out for a whole week."

"Isabelle?" asked Sam, as he ripped off some paper towels and mopped up the milk puddle on the floor.

"Hurricane, son. Ever noticed the floodwall downtown? They didn't build it to keep out Yankees like you, although that's not such a bad idea. It's for the water. Of course, nothing's hit us like Agnes in '72."

Dad returned from the garage carrying two thick, yellow extension cords. "Think these will do the trick, Jonas?"

"Bingo. You sure you can spare 'em?" Mr. Haskins pointed out the deck door. "I can probably run one over here to juice your fridge as well."

"That would be nice of you, thanks," said Dad, just as the room filled with light.

"Power's on!" Derek shouted.

Sam shook his head. "Thanks, genius."

"Figures." Mr. Haskins grunted. "I'm always prepared when I don't need it." He stood, holding out his extension cords. "Well, at least I'll be ready for the next one."

"Caitlin's parents picked her up, I assume?" Mom asked as Dad walked Mr. Haskins to the door.

"Yeah," said Sam, "but we need to talk to you about something else."

Dad walked back in and raised an eyebrow. "What do we need to talk about?"

Sam bit his lip and eyed his brother. "You talked to him."

"I think you guys had better sit down," said Derek, repeating his warning from earlier. Then he explained about the collect call from the prison. Mom's eyes looked like they were about to pop out of her head.

Everyone was silent for a moment. Dad nodded at the clock. "Maybe we've had enough excitement for one night. Let's all get some sleep and we can talk about this more in the morning. But I'm glad you told us."

"You think we're safe tonight?" asked Sam. As much as he felt foolish for being scared by Mr. Haskins, hearing that Jerry was out of jail and plotting against them still made him worried.

"Yes," said Dad. "But if it will make you feel better, I'll double-check that the doors are locked."

"Thanks," said Sam.

"He'd better just hope that he doesn't meet me first," said Derek, throwing a series of quick punches in the air on his way upstairs. "He'll be wishing he was back in the slammer by the time I'm done with him."

"Sure he will," said Sam.

CHAPTER SIXTEEN

The next morning, Sam woke later than usual. His stomach growled, and he hoped it was pancake day. His mom made the best banana pancakes with a sprinkle of chocolate chips. They were delicious.

He dressed and found his parents and Derek already downstairs.

"Morning."

"Good morning, sweetie," Mom answered. "How'd you sleep?"

"Not so good."

"Bad dreams?"

He nodded. "A few." Jerry had returned to his dreams again. Like before, he'd been back at St. John's Church, creeping through the stone basement where Jerry had grabbed him.

Another growl from his stomach turned his thoughts back to breakfast. "Can we have pancakes today?"

"I can probably manage that."

"Banana? With chocolate chips?"

Mom raised her eyebrows and waited for him to continue.

"Please?"

She nodded with a smile. "Coming right up."

"We can chat in the meantime," said Dad, sitting between the boys at the table.

"Uh-oh," moaned Derek. "That's never good."

"Did you call the cops?" asked Sam.

Derek shook his head. "Why would we call the cops?"

Sam glared back at his brother. "Because of the *phone call*. Remember? I know I didn't just dream that Jerry's coming after us." Sometimes he wondered if they were living in the same house.

"No one said he's actually coming after us," said Derek. "It was just a heads-up."

Sam's jaw dropped open. "Any time I get a heads-up from prison, I count that as a bad thing." Was he the only one who thought that was a problem?

"And you're sure that man, Jerry, hasn't tried to contact either of you?" asked Dad, eyeing them across the table. "I need the truth. This isn't the time to keep secrets."

Sam shook his head. "Not me. Just Ben's call last night." He stared back at his brother. "From *prison*!"

"I'll call down to my friend Mark at the police station and see what he thinks," said Dad. "But I'm not sure there's much he can do based on a secondhand comment."

"I want both of you to be careful," said Mom.

"Of course," said Derek. "That's my middle name." He looked at Sam. "Actually, it's also Sam's first name."

Sam didn't know what the police could do about it either, but he was happy to stay away from Jerry and whatever evil schemes he had up his sleeve. His phone buzzed with a text from Caitlin.

Meet at the creek in 30 mins?

"Another message from prison, or just your girl-friend?" said Derek.

Sam ignored him and texted Caitlin back.

Cool. Cu there

Sam knew she wanted to make more plans about going to Poplar Forest. Ever since she'd first read that journal, she'd had a determined look in her eye. She wasn't going to let this go until she found the answers she was searching for. He thought about mentioning the whole mystery to his parents, but he knew Derek wouldn't want him to.

* * *

AS HE ENTERED the dark canopy of the trees at the end of their yard, Sam sensed he wasn't alone. He glanced over his shoulder and saw Derek's goofy grin. He was trailing behind him like a dog that wouldn't go home. Caitlin had climbed halfway across a wide log that had fallen across the creek and waved as she waited for the boys to get closer. Her shoes sat next to her, and she dangled one foot down just above the water.

"Hey!" she called.

"Hope you don't mind, I brought Sam along," Derek answered quickly.

"You brought me—" Sam started before realizing he was falling right into his brother's trap.

Caitlin laughed. "I'm glad you're both here. We need to make a decision."

"About?" said Derek.

She pulled out a slip of paper. "About Aubrey."

Sam closed his eyes. "I thought we'd already decided that she wasn't trustworthy. We don't need her. She needs us, remember?"

"I think *you* decided that, Sam." Derek gathered a handful of pebbles from the edge of the creek and tossed them at a tree with a thud. "*We* said we still need to get to Poplar Forest."

"Dad said we should stay close to home after last night," said Sam. "We might have to forget about the clues for a while."

"Last night?" asked Caitlin.

Sam's jaw dropped open. "You too? Doesn't anybody else think it's important that we got a death threat from prison? What's the matter with you guys?"

"It wasn't a death threat, Sam," said Derek.

"Practically."

"Don't you think you're being a little dramatic?" Caitlin splashed water up at him with her toe.

Sam put his hands on his hips and glared at her. "I don't think this is a great time for another road trip, letter or no letter. How are we going to explain where we're going? We met some random girl at Monticello and now she wants to give us a ride? Oh, and by the way, she's the one who stole the journal from the bookstore."

"She gave it back," said Derek.

Sam spread his arms wide. "Oh, well, that makes it all okay."

"She seemed sorry," said Caitlin, pulling her shoes back on. She stood, balancing herself on the log. "I think we should forgive her."

"Sure," said Sam. "Why don't you try that at the bank. Steal a few thousand bucks, then give it back a few days later and see if all is forgiven. It doesn't work that way."

"This isn't quite the same," said Caitlin, hopping down next to him on the creek bank. "I think she sincerely wants to work together. She has a real interest in history, and we don't run into that every day. And what about Nelly and Ellie?"

"What about them?"

"I can't just forget about what we read in their letters. I think they came to me for a reason."

"They *came to you*?" Sam frowned.

"You know what I mean." She held out the paper with Aubrey's phone number. "We can at least call her."

Sam sighed. It seemed like, in times like these, it didn't matter what he said. When Derek and Caitlin got their minds set on something, he was outnumbered. "Fine. But I don't like it."

"What a surprise," muttered Derek.

"Great." Caitlin pulled out her phone and dialed the number. She placed the call on speaker and held it between them as it rang.

"Hello?"

"Aubrey?" said Caitlin.

"Speaking."

"Hi," said Derek, leaning closer. It was nearly impossible in situations like these for him to keep his mouth shut. "It's Derek and Caitlin from the other day."

Sam nudged him in the arm.

"Oh, and Sam's here too."

"Oh, hi, guys," Aubrey answered. "I'm glad you called."

"We've been considering your offer to work together," said Caitlin. "Do you think you could drive us to Poplar Forest? I mean, if you're free."

"Yeah, totally," Aubrey said. "That's awesome. How about this afternoon? I can get a friend to cover for me at work."

Sam groaned. This afternoon was fast. They hadn't even come up with an explanation for their parents about where they were going.

"Uh…" Caitlin glanced past Sam, who was shaking

his head. Derek nodded enthusiastically. "Sure, I guess that will work," she answered.

"Great plan," Sam grumbled after she'd coordinated the details and hung up. "You think Mom and Dad will say yes?" He turned to Caitlin. "Or your parents?"

"You think they'll notice if we're gone?" asked Derek.

Caitlin chuckled. "I think I have an idea."

"I have an idea too." Sam stood and turned toward home.

"Where are you going now?" called Derek.

"Sam," said Caitlin. "Don't leave."

He stopped and looked back at them. "You two can go with your new friend on your crazy wild goose chase. Have a great time! I hope you find lots more letters about fairy palaces."

He spun on his heel and continued walking up the hill toward their yard. "I'm staying here!"

"Sam, don't be like that," Caitlin called after him, but he didn't turn around. He'd had enough. Maybe it was the phone call the night before, or all the bad memories about Jerry that it had stirred up within him, but he wasn't just going to give in this time. He didn't care what they said.

CHAPTER SEVENTEEN

The blue coupe stopped at the top of the cul-de-sac where Caitlin and Derek were waiting. Aubrey lowered the window and smiled at them, strands of her red hair blowing in the wind. "Ready?"

"Hey," said Derek, opening the passenger door. "You can ride up front, Caitlin." Aubrey reached over and folded the seat forward so Derek could climb into the back seat.

"Thanks," Caitlin said. She turned to Aubrey as she buckled up. "And thanks for the ride."

"No problem," Aubrey replied. "Where's your brother? Isn't he coming too?"

Derek groaned. "He's not feeling up to it."

"But the three of us should be able to handle things," said Caitlin.

"That's too bad," said Aubrey. "You two didn't have trouble getting away?"

Caitlin shifted uncomfortably in her seat. "We came up with an excuse."

"Awesome. I was hoping you might call. I knew we'd be a good match." She pulled onto the main road and headed west. "We've got a couple hours here in the car. I'm hoping that we can compare notes along the way. You're okay with that, right?"

Caitlin nodded. She'd cooked up a story that she and Derek were going to Julie Miller's vacation house on Lake Anna. Ordinarily, Caitlin and Derek doing something together on their own would have raised suspicion, but Julie's older brother, Tony, was Derek's age, so it provided the perfect cover. Lake Anna was an hour north, but their true destination, Poplar Forest, was two hours west.

She didn't like lying to her parents, and she felt bad that Sam wasn't coming too. She hated being at odds with anyone, let alone a best friend like Sam. But she couldn't let this opportunity pass them by. Now that they were literally headed down the road with Aubrey, it only made sense to tell her what they knew.

"Well, you've read the journal, obviously, so you know Ellie and Nelly were talking about hidden treasure."

Aubrey glanced over at her. "Ellie and Nelly?"

"Sorry." Caitlin chuckled. "I keep forgetting that doesn't make sense to everyone else. That's what I nicknamed Ellen and Cornelia. You know, Jefferson's granddaughters. I feel like I know them after reading their letters."

"She gets really into this stuff," said Derek, leaning between the front seats.

Aubrey smiled. "I like that! I'll start calling them Ellie and Nelly too." She glanced at Derek in the rearview mirror. "It can be a girl thing."

Caitlin beamed. It had taken her a while to get past their rocky start from the bookstore, but Aubrey seemed fun. Even after such a short time, she could tell they were going to be friends. She might even end up like a big sister.

"That was what first caught my attention too," Aubrey said. "The treasure. I've always thought that part of history was interesting, when Jefferson had to flee Monticello. But I didn't imagine some of it might still be missing, and I don't know what the collection is either."

"After seeing the house up close, I can see why he was reluctant to leave," said Caitlin.

"Thank goodness for the cuckoo guy," said Derek.

"Is that another nickname?" asked Aubrey.

Caitlin shook her head. "I think he means Jack Jouett. It was the Cuckoo Tavern, Derek. *He* wasn't cuckoo."

"Same difference. You knew what I meant."

Aubrey laughed. "You guys are too much. My roommate is always going on about how she has fun with her younger brothers and sisters at home. You remind me of her stories. I don't have any siblings, so I never quite got it."

Caitlin's eyes bugged wide. "Oh my gosh, me too! I mean, I'm an only child too."

Aubrey reached over and gave Caitlin a high five. "It's like we have a special bond, girl."

"Okay, enough with the girl power," Derek grumbled.

Caitlin laughed. "You're just not used to being outnumbered. Now you know how I feel."

"Yeah, yeah," said Derek. "So tell me this, how did Cuckoo Jack know that the British were coming?"

"Well," said Caitlin. "I read about that on the car ride home from Monticello. Jouett saw the British solders arrive at the tavern and overheard them talking about attacking Charlottesville. The legislature had moved there in fear that the British would overtake Richmond."

"Which they did," said Aubrey.

Caitlin nodded. "Right. So when Jouett heard their plans to capture Jefferson and the legislature, he rode through the night to warn them all. He followed the Three Chopt Road, a trail marked by three notches cut in the trees, and reached Monticello just before dawn."

"He must have hightailed it out of there," said Derek.

"Well, he had a little help," said Aubrey. "When Lieutenant Colonel Tarleton and his men stopped for breakfast along the way, the owners of the place where they were eating kept messing up the meal to stall them from heading out toward Charlottesville."

Caitlin laughed. "Really? I didn't know that part."

"Yep. My dad told me about that," said Aubrey. "He's a big Jefferson fan. Another crazy thing is that when

Jouett arrived, Jefferson didn't seem to believe he was really in danger. He thought Monticello would be safe. He kind of dillydallied for a while."

"Dillydallied?" said Derek. "Is that an official presidential thing to do?"

Aubrey laughed. "Maybe not, but remember, this all happened before he became president. He was ending his term as governor."

"So he didn't leave Monticello?" asked Derek. "Was he captured?"

Caitlin shook her head. "No, he left eventually. Just not right away. After Jouett warned him, he finished breakfast and sent his family away in a carriage. He rode his horse to the top of the mountain next to Monticello and looked through his folding telescope. The legend says that at first he didn't see the soldiers coming. He was about to ride back home, but he accidentally dropped his sword, and when he leaned down to pick it up, he saw the sunlight reflecting off the uniforms of the British solders coming up the mountain. He rode off just minutes before one of Tarleton's men—"

"Captain McLeod," said Aubrey.

"Before Captain McLeod reached Monticello."

"Wow, that really was a close one," said Derek. "But what about the treasure? Don't tell me Sam was right and we're just looking for fairy palaces."

"Before he left, Jefferson stuffed papers where he could," said Caitlin, enjoying the chance to share everything she'd learned. It was like she and Aubrey were teaching a lesson. "Then he ordered Martin Hemings to hide the valuables."

"That's who the journal mentioned," said Derek.

Caitlin nodded. "Exactly."

"When McLeod arrived with his men, Martin was hiding everything," said Aubrey. "McLeod pointed a gun to his chest and demanded he say where Jefferson had gone."

"Did he tell him?" asked Derek.

Aubrey shook her head. "Nope."

"He was brave," said Derek. "I'll bet I wouldn't have talked either."

"It was very loyal, too," said Aubrey, "especially since a lot of slaves had defected when the British promised to grant their freedom."

"So why didn't he?" asked Derek. "Gaining your freedom would be pretty hard to pass up, even if you were a slave for somebody like Jefferson."

"We don't know," Aubrey replied. "But I have a question for you two."

"Shoot," said Derek.

"Why were you hiding in the Cuddy? Was there something hidden there? I didn't see anything in the Dome Room."

Caitlin pulled out the letter that had fallen from the journal and read it to Aubrey. She explained how Sam had found the loose brick beneath the boards. At the next red light, she showed Aubrey the picture on her phone of the note and the drawing. "That's why we're heading to Poplar Forest."

"Wow," said Aubrey. "I knew you must have something good."

"Why didn't you bust us?" asked Derek. "Sam said you saw him hiding."

Aubrey grinned. "Tell your brother he needs to hide behind a bigger sofa next time. I didn't say anything because I sensed we could work together. I figured if you were hiding in there, you must know more than I did." She tapped her hand on the steering wheel. "And I think I might know the kitchen they're talking about at Poplar Forest."

"You do?" said Caitlin.

Aubrey nodded. "When they excavated the wing next to the house, they uncovered the remains of several workrooms. I think one of them was a kitchen."

"You've seen it?" asked Derek.

"Not yet, but I'm on their email list. They have a blog that shows recent discoveries and how the archaeologists work."

"Impressive," said Derek.

Aubrey looked back at him and grinned. "I told you, I'm into this stuff. Plus, it's a little easier when you don't have to get permission from your parents."

Derek sighed. "That day can't come soon enough."

"What's it like to go to school at Thomas Jefferson's university?" asked Caitlin. "It must be awesome."

"So far it's been great. Believe it or not, you kind of

get used to seeing all the history around, although I guess there are more tourists than at other schools. I wasn't sure if I'd get in, but I received a partial scholarship."

"Your parents must have been happy about that," said Caitlin. She was still several years from college, but her parents were already talking about how expensive it would be when she did go.

"Oh sure. My folks are divorced, and I lived with my mom in high school, so it was hard to move out and leave her. But I learned a lot about history from my dad."

"Does he live near here?" asked Caitlin.

Aubrey shrugged. "Not really. I see him on short visits sometimes, but he's pretty busy."

"You said this was his car?" asked Derek.

Aubrey nodded. "Yeah, but he let me use it when I left for school."

"Is he a doctor?"

"No, why?"

"Sam was trying to figure out the license plate," said Caitlin. "It ends in MD, so he thought it might belong to a doctor."

Aubrey laughed. "No, but that's a good guess. I don't think it means anything."

The time passed quickly, and soon they turned onto a side road and down a long gravel driveway.

"Is this it?" asked Derek.

"I think so," said Aubrey as they drove toward a wide, circular driveway flanked by towering trees that surrounded a redbrick house.

CHAPTER EIGHTEEN

Poplar Forest was like visiting Monticello, but on a smaller scale. Which made sense, Caitlin thought, since Thomas Jefferson had built it years after constructing his main home back in Charlottesville. It was simplified, like a country house would be, but with some of the same basic architectural features that Jefferson had learned over the years.

"I don't see a dome," said Derek.

"There's not one, I don't think," said Aubrey. "But just like Monticello's Dome Room, this entire house is in the shape of an octagon."

Derek's expression perked up. "It's like MMA."

"MMA?" asked Caitlin.

"You know, mixed martial arts. They fight in an octagon ring so you can't hide in the corners."

Aubrey laughed. "I'm pretty sure Jefferson didn't fight, but he liked his rooms angled so there weren't dark corners." She looked back at Derek. "But Abraham Lincoln might have liked your idea."

"Lincoln?" said Derek. "What's he have to do with it?"

"He was a big wrestler when he was younger."

"Really?" Caitlin raised her eyebrows. "Or are you just making that up?"

"It's true," said Aubrey. "He's in the wrestling hall of fame. Look it up."

"I'll do that," said Derek.

"But first, let's find the answers to our clue," said Caitlin as they walked toward the small, red visitor center building on the other side of the parking lot. The sign outside the door said the last entry was at 4:00, and it was already 3:30. "We'd better hurry."

They bought three self-guided tour passes and rushed across the wide lawn. Derek pointed to two narrow outbuildings positioned symmetrically several yards from both ends of the house. "Are those guard booths?"

"I think those are necessaries," said Aubrey.

Derek lowered his eyebrows. "Necessary for what?"

She laughed. "Necessary for going to the bathroom. They're outdoor toilets. In Jefferson's time they were called necessaries, or privies."

Derek made a funny face. "That's weird."

Aubrey shrugged. "Not for them."

Stone pillars decorated the front porch just like at Monticello, but the inside felt completely different from Mr. Jefferson's main home. Some of the walls looked recently plastered, and several rooms still had bare brick walls. Wide wooden beams supported the roof above their heads. The style was familiar, but instead of a decorated mansion filled to the brim with artifacts, bookcases, musical instruments, and fine furniture, the house was sparsely furnished.

Derek whistled. "Looks like somebody cleaned them out."

"I think it's supposed to be this way," said Aubrey.

"Maybe he tried to keep it simple," said Caitlin. She stopped and read aloud an informational sign with a quote from Jefferson. *"I visit three or four times a year, and stay from a fortnight to a month at a time."*

"*Fortnite*!?" Derek's head jerked up. "He played video games too?"

"Stop," Caitlin said. She thought Derek's jokes were funny most of the time, but now they needed to hurry and look for clues. But it was nearly impossible not to take a few moments to look around. It wouldn't take long. There was no upstairs, only a series of connecting angled rooms that surrounded a large dining room in the very center of the house. The dining room was the only square-shaped room, and while the elevated ceiling wasn't capped in a dome, a long, rectangular skylight ran high above them.

"It's so pretty," Caitlin marveled. Skylights seemed to run a close second to domes on Jefferson's list of favorite architectural features.

"Let's go outside," said Aubrey, leading them out to a

long terrace. A guide was explaining to an older couple that the terrace covered a series of smaller working rooms, which Jefferson had called his Wing of Offices.

"Jefferson visited Poplar Forest for the last time in the spring of 1823," the woman said. "At his death three years later, he left the estate to his grandson Francis Eppes and his wife, who had been living here for several years."

"Not a bad inheritance," Derek muttered.

The guide smiled at them. "Except they didn't seem to like it. They quickly sold Poplar Forest and moved to Florida. Amazingly, families still lived here until the early 1980s, when it was purchased by our nonprofit group."

"Excuse me," said Caitlin. "You said his grandson lived here, but what about his granddaughters? I read that they visited a lot, too."

"Very true," answered the woman, whose name tag said Linda. She pointed to the corner of the terrace. "You'll probably be very interested in that sign."

Caitlin caught her breath as she saw an informational sign. The writing was an excerpt of a letter—from Ellie!

We saw, too, more of our dear grandfather at those times than at any other… He interested himself in all we did, thought or read. He would talk to us about his own youth and early friends and tell us stories of former days. He seemed really to take as much pleasure in these conversations with us, as if we had been older and wiser people. - Ellen Randolph

Caitlin stared across the terrace at several enormous trees along the circular driveway. Poplars, she guessed, and from their size, they must have been there during Jefferson's time at the home. That would make them over two hundred years old! She could almost imagine being here with her grandfather, watching the daylight slowly fade over the horizon. After everything Jefferson had experienced in his life, it must have been a very peaceful way to relax. She could tell why he'd liked it here.

"We'll be closing up shortly," Linda called as she walked back inside.

"But we haven't found anything yet," said Derek. "Where's the kitchen?"

Aubrey pointed at a brick chimney protruding up through the terrace floor. "I think it's right below us." They took stairs off the terrace onto the grass. A row of small rooms had entrances from the lawn. Most of the floors were stone or dirt and seemed like they'd been recently excavated.

"These don't seem like offices," said Derek. "More like workrooms."

Caitlin poked her head into the next room. "Here's the kitchen." She stepped into the dark, brick room, but it was hard to know exactly what she was looking at. She pulled out her phone and compared the picture of the drawing to the room. They didn't look the same at all.

"This isn't right," she muttered. The remains of a fireplace were on one side, but she couldn't see how things would line up with the drawing.

"How are we supposed to find a clue in here?" asked Derek, looking over her shoulder.

"I don't know." She held her phone up to Aubrey. "Does it look the same to you?"

"Not really," Aubrey answered, looking back and forth from the phone to the room.

"Can I help you kids with anything else?" Linda asked from the doorway. "We're about to close up."

"Is this the kitchen?" asked Caitlin.

"It is. These rooms next to the main house were storage, a kitchen, the smokehouse, and most likely living quarters. They had at one point been rebuilt as separate buildings, but our researchers uncovered some of the original brick floors, stone hearths, and wall foundations that allowed them to restore it close to the original."

Caitlin's face sank. That explained the differences from the drawing. How were they supposed to find a clue if the part of the house they were looking for wasn't even here anymore?

"That's not good," said Derek.

"When were those changes made?" asked Aubrey.

"Oh, about twenty years ago now. You might look at the displays in the basement, where we have some artifacts that the archeologists discovered during their efforts."

Caitlin raised her head. "Artifacts?"

"Sure," said Linda. "Many items were uncovered during excavations... pottery, coins, eating utensils, nails, all sorts of things."

"Can we see them?" asked Aubrey.

Linda checked her watch. "Yes, but you'll need to be quick." She led them over to a brick basement with the wide, wooden floorboards of the main house overhead. A sunken area in the center of the room was labeled the wine cellar.

"See anything?" asked Derek, pointing to a glass display case along the wall. It reminded Caitlin of the Archaerium at Jamestown where they'd found many artifacts from the original English settlers. She saw loads of interesting objects, but nothing that hinted at a connection to the letters or the drawing. She held the picture on her phone. What was she missing?

"Isn't that interesting?"

Caitlin jumped in surprise. Linda was standing right behind her, looking over her shoulder. "It's supposed to be a drawing of Jefferson's kitchen. But I think we're at a dead end."

"Do you mind if I take a look?" Linda asked.

"Um, sure." Caitlin handed over her phone. Derek looked over at her skeptically, but Caitlin just shrugged. It would be rude to say no.

"Well, that's your problem, now isn't it," Linda proclaimed.

"What?" asked Aubrey.

"Do you recognize something?" asked Caitlin.

"Why sure," Linda answered, holding out the phone. "You're at the wrong kitchen. The writing speaks of enjoying James's French cuisine, when of course James

Hemings wasn't here at Poplar Forest. He was Jefferson's chef at Monticello."

Caitlin's mouth dropped open.

"She's right," exclaimed Aubrey. "How did I miss that?"

"Where did you find that picture?" Linda asked.

"It's kind of a long story," said Derek.

"Is there a kitchen that looks like that picture at Monticello?" asked Caitlin.

Linda nodded. "Actually, they've recently unearthed the original kitchen in Monticello's South Pavilion. It's the building at the end of the wing. Monticello has two wings, of course, where we here at Poplar Forest only have one." She stopped to think, then held up her finger. "In fact, if you follow me, I think this might prove my point." She walked around to the other side of the basement to a different display board. She pointed to a pencil sketch of a square room that was labeled "South Pavilion kitchen plans, 1770."

Caitlin held up her phone and gasped. It was a perfect match. The only difference was the small compartment next to the fireplace. That had to be where the treasure was.

"You mean all this time, it's been right there at Monticello?" asked Derek in disbelief.

"It looks like it," said Aubrey.

Caitlin turned and hugged Linda. "I can't thank you enough! If we find anything, we'll be sure to let you know."

Linda chuckled. "That's what I'm here for."

Derek reached out and shook her hand. "You're a darned good docent, Linda."

Aubrey typed something into her phone then pointed toward the parking lot. "We need to get going."

"Going where?" asked Caitlin.

Aubrey smiled mischievously. "To Monticello. Do you want to solve this thing or not?"

CHAPTER NINETEEN

S am had watched Derek and Caitlin slip into Aubrey's blue car at the top of the cul-de-sac from his bedroom window. He shook his head as it sped off, debating his decision. It seemed no matter what he did, Derek would poke fun at him or make it seem like he was chicken. He'd had enough of Derek's comments about shirt slogans and the other teardowns. Sam just didn't want to deal with any more of those right now, but he was also used to that stuff coming from Derek. What bothered him more was that Caitlin had sided with Derek over him.

Sam wondered if Caitlin was regretting going as much as he was regretting staying. As far as he knew, she never lied to her parents, but she'd become obsessed with discovering what Jefferson's granddaughters were writing about. Sam was curious too, but ever since the phone call about Jerry, he couldn't get his head straight.

He closed the sports magazine he'd been using to distract himself and tossed it on the floor. He'd been reading a baseball article about Thurman Munson, the old Yankees catcher who was killed in a plane crash in the middle of the season. It was interesting but depressing at the same time. And the last thing he needed was more depressing things to think about.

Now he was just bored. He thought about calling to check in, but couldn't bring himself to do it. That defeated the purpose of staying home.

A knock sounded at his door. "Sam?"

"In here."

Dad peeked his head in and walked over to him. "Whatcha doing?"

"Nothing."

"Wishing you were at the lake with Derek?"

"Kinda."

"Anything you want to talk about?"

Sam pulled his pillow over his head. "No," he said in a muffled voice. "I'm fine."

"I can see that." Dad slid the pillow away. "This doesn't have anything to do with that phone call, does it?"

"No." Sam let out a long sigh. "Well, maybe."

"Despite what your brother might tell you, there's no shame in being a little scared," said Dad. "You had a pretty traumatic ordeal with that guy. It would stick in my head as well if I'd been in your shoes."

"You think?"

"Absolutely." Dad picked the magazine up off the floor and set it on Sam's nightstand. "What were you reading about?"

"Thurman Munson."

Dad gave a solemn smile. "Quite a ballplayer."

Sam sat up and leaned against the wall. "Did you watch him play?"

"Well, he played forty years ago, so I was just a little kid and don't really remember it. But I've heard Grandpa talk about him all my life. He was the team captain, you know."

"Yeah. It must have been hard for his teammates."

"Especially his close friends. The whole team flew to Ohio for the funeral and then had to play a game that night in New York against Baltimore. His best friend, Bobby Murcer, fought back tears when he spoke at the funeral. That night, he hit a three-run homer in the fifth and then won the game with a two-run, walk-off single in the ninth."

"That's incredible," said Sam. "It must have been hard for him to do."

Dad nodded. "No doubt. But somehow he made it through."

"That's a lot worse than what I'm dealing with."

"It's different, but I'm confident that you'll be able to work through your situation too." Dad stood and walked to the doorway. "The reason I came up here was to let you know that Mom and I are about to leave."

"Right." Sam had forgotten about that when he chose

to stay home. Dad had surprised Mom with tickets to a musical for her birthday. They were going downtown with Caitlin's parents.

"You'll be okay?"

"Sure."

"Mom's leaving you a dinner plate in the microwave. We won't be reachable for a couple hours during the performance, but I told Mr. Haskins next door you'll be here by yourself. You can check with him if you have an emergency."

Sam rolled his eyes. "He's more likely to need *me* than I am him."

Dad chuckled. "Probably so."

"Hey Dad, any idea what *GMLOGMD* stands for?"

"Um…" His dad thought about it for a few seconds. "Don't think I know that one… Good music lets ordinary goofy men dance?"

Sam made a face. That was worse than what he'd come up with. "Never mind."

He told his parents goodbye from the front door and watched the end of a TV show while eating his dinner. Once that finished, there was nothing else to do, so he walked into the kitchen and pulled out a blank sheet of paper and a pencil.

GMLOGMD

He worked the letters around in his head.

Guys might lose our gloves making doughnuts.

The phone rang, the landline, and for a moment Sam froze. The last time that phone had rung it was the collect call from prison. Was Ben calling back with another warning? Maybe this time it was Jerry himself calling. Sam almost didn't want to answer it, but he remembered Bobby Murcer and forced himself to do the hard thing.

"Hello?" he almost whispered.

"Did you know life insurance is the best way to protect your loved ones in the event of an untimely death?" a salesman's voice nearly shouted at him.

Sam shook his head. "How'd you like an untimely death?!" he yelled back, slamming the phone down. He hated telemarketers. That was now two things in a row talking about death—Thurman Munson's funeral, and life insurance, whatever that was. He thought again about Munson.

Golden moments loom over great man's death

He circled the last word. Death. He couldn't imagine one of his favorite ballplayers dying. He started writing a new phrase without even thinking about it.

… give me death…

Another phrase popped into his head. The letters fit.

Give me liberty or give me death…

Hey, it was just like the famous line from Patrick Henry that they'd heard at St. John's Church. He dropped the pencil onto the floor.

"Oh my gosh," he said aloud.

CHAPTER TWENTY

Caitlin's phone rang as she rode in the back seat of Aubrey's car. "It's Sam."

Derek snickered. "A little late to change his mind."

"Hello?" Caitlin listened but there was only static on the line. "Sam?" She glanced at the screen but her phone only had one bar of service. She couldn't hear anything. "Sam, I'll have to call you back. We're in the mountains, I think."

"Too bad he couldn't come," said Aubrey.

"He would have liked it," agreed Caitlin.

"Sam gets way too nervous about most things," said Derek. He told Aubrey about the T-shirt.

"That's mean."

Derek shrugged. "It's true."

"You don't always have to say things, even if they are true," said Caitlin.

"Maybe," said Derek. "You sound like my mom."

Probably because she's smart, thought Caitlin. But she tried to listen to her own advice and said nothing.

Aubrey glanced at her GPS. "I didn't ask, but are you both going to be okay staying away a little longer?"

"We've come this far," said Derek.

"Caitlin?"

"Yeah, it's fine."

Derek leaned forward to see the green road sign over the highway overpass. "How far is it to Monticello?"

"About an hour and a half," said Aubrey. "Although, it took Jefferson three days to travel this route."

"Did he walk?" asked Derek.

"No," said Aubrey. "He traveled on horseback or by carriage."

Derek reached forward and nudged Caitlin's shoulder. "Surprised you didn't know that one."

"Yeah," she replied.

"Are you okay?" asked Aubrey.

"Just a little tired, I guess," Caitlin answered. For once, she didn't feel like going on about Thomas Jefferson's travel methods. She'd said she was fine, but she didn't feel quite right. Her parents would be expecting her back at some point soon. She knew they were downtown at the musical, but she sent them a quick text saying they were staying longer at the lake than they'd expected. She tried to ignore the guilt that crept into her brain and reminded herself it would all be worth it when they found the treasure.

Just outside Charlottesville, Aubrey's phone rang. She

held it up to her ear as she drove. "Hi… yeah, we're getting close… okay, sounds good."

She hung up and glanced over at them. "That was my dad."

"I thought you said he was away," said Derek.

Aubrey nodded. "Most of the time. He's home for a while now, though. I texted him that we might find something at Monticello and he asked if he could meet us there. I told you he's a big history buff too."

Caitlin didn't know how she felt about Aubrey's dad joining them. Working with a college-age student like Aubrey was one thing. She was a few years older than them, but she still didn't really seem like an adult. Discovering things with her felt just like being with Sam and Derek. But Mom and Dad already thought she was at the lake, and they wouldn't be happy to find out she had lied to them and was working with a grown-up man who was a stranger, even if he was Aubrey's dad.

Aubrey pulled into a rest stop in front of several small, brick buildings with restrooms and vending machines. "I'm getting a granola bar. You guys want anything?"

Caitlin realized she should probably eat something. There was no telling how long they'd be at Monticello. Maybe some food would help her feel better. "Sure. Thanks."

"I'm going to use the necessary," said Derek.

"Good idea," said Caitlin. "Me too."

After she used the restroom, Caitlin read one of the

tall information boards for visitors that was posted along the sidewalk. It featured a map of Virginia and several nearby points of interest like Monticello.

Headlights pulled into the parking lot on the other side of the sign Caitlin was reading. She leaned around the board and squinted through the dusk to see a man behind the wheel. She was about to head back to the car but then jerked back behind the board.

Even in the fading light, she recognized the man's face. Her heart raced as she pressed up against the wooden board.

It was Jerry.

What was he doing here? She couldn't see Aubrey and the vending machine pavilion, but Derek walked out of the men's restroom. She held her finger in front of her lips and waved him over behind the sign.

"We have to get out of here," she whispered.

"Why? What's wrong?"

"It's Jerry!"

Derek's eyes widened. "Jerry? Here? Are you sure?"

Caitlin nodded. "He's in that car over there." She pointed across the parking lot to his car. His trunk was open, and he was pulling something out.

"Where's Aubrey?"

"Still by the vending machines, I think." Caitlin leaned around the edge of the sign and looked toward the pavilion. Aubrey emerged with her hands full of snacks. She headed for the parking lot just as Jerry closed his trunk. A long, thin, metal object like a tire iron or a crowbar was in his right hand. He was heading right for her!

"He must be following us," said Derek, springing forward. "We have to warn her."

They moved from behind the sign, but just as they reached the edge of the parking lot, Aubrey turned around. Jerry's hand rose like he would strike her. Caitlin tried to call out, but her throat was suddenly dry and she couldn't get the words out. But then his arm lowered gently on Aubrey's shoulder. He pulled her into an embrace.

Caitlin and Derek both froze. Everything came together in Caitlin's mind like it was suddenly in fast-forward. Aubrey looked at them, just twenty feet away in the middle of the parking lot. She said something to Jerry, and they both began walking over.

"Oh my gosh," Caitlin whispered.

"You've got to be kidding me," said Derek.

Aubrey's face looked friendly but serious as she stopped a couple of yards from Derek and Caitlin with Jerry at her side. "I'd introduce you to my father, but I think you've already met."

Caitlin didn't know what to say. It all made sense now. Why this girl had come out of nowhere, stolen the journal from her mom's bookstore, and then strangely befriended them. Her dad had been away. He loved history. Caitlin closed her eyes. It had been right in front of her all along. How could she have been so blind?

"What a surprise to see you two again," said Jerry, a

smile plastered on his face. He glanced around the parking lot. "But where's your brother? Don't tell me the Three Musketeers broke up?"

"He stayed at home," explained Aubrey.

Jerry clucked his tongue. "That's a shame. I thought we'd have the whole band together again."

It had been a few years since the police had led Jerry away in cuffs at Colonial Williamsburg. Caitlin knew he'd been sentenced to prison, but she'd hoped it would have been for longer than this. His dark hair and trimmed beard showed flecks of gray, but otherwise, he hadn't changed much.

"No matter," said Jerry. "It's still quite the coincidence for us to be on the same historical path again."

"I doubt that," said Caitlin.

"What do you want?" asked Derek. "And how'd you get out of prison so fast?"

"I served my time. Released early on good behavior, actually." Jerry crossed his arms. "I've had quite a bit of time to think since the last time we were all together. And while I will confess, I haven't always harbored the fondest affections for the three of you, there's a bit of admiration that accompanies any defeat. I think we all share something in common."

"You enjoy seeing yourself behind bars too?" asked Derek.

Jerry ignored him. "A love of history."

"Love?" cried Caitlin. "You're just a thief. Both of

you." She tried to read Aubrey's face, but it revealed nothing. "All this time, you were just playing us?"

Aubrey shrugged. "Not all of it. I really do like history. But I'm just a little more interested in finding the treasure than I am in being friends with some kids. No hard feelings."

"Oh sure," Derek replied. "We'll just add you to the Christmas card list."

"I told you we were meeting my father. I didn't lie about anything."

Derek shook his head. "You probably knew who we were from the beginning. Is that the only reason you talked to us?"

"Let's just say, acting runs in the family," Aubrey answered.

"I can see you still harbor bad feelings toward me," said Jerry, "so let's get down to business, shall we?"

"We don't have any business with you," said Caitlin. "You nearly killed us." She didn't know why he was trying to sweet-talk them, but it would not work. They couldn't believe anything he said.

"I told you he was into finding lost things from history," said Aubrey. "We all want the same thing. To find the treasure."

"I don't know what you're talking about," said Caitlin.

Jerry rolled his eyes. "If you were any other kids I might believe that, but I've followed enough of your exploits to know better." Jerry's eyes narrowed. "We all know there's a treasure on Jefferson's mountain. Aubrey tells me you've found the location in the South Pavilion."

"What if we have?" asked Derek.

Jerry grinned and held up the crowbar. "This is one treasure that I don't intend to leave without."

"So what do you need us for?" asked Caitlin.

Jerry's expression turned ice cold. "Nothing."

Caitlin's frustration quickly turned to fear. Her chest suddenly felt tight. This was all going wrong. Sam was right; it was all too dangerous. She should never have lied to her parents. No one knew where they were. Even Sam thought they were at Poplar Forest, not Monticello. She thought of screaming, but the rest of the parking lot was deserted.

"But," sighed Jerry, "I can't exactly leave you standing here waiting for the next tourist to drive up. So you'll just have to come with us." He pointed to Aubrey's car. "Get in."

They both hesitated when Aubrey opened the door, but what were they going to do? Derek was strong, but he probably still wasn't a match for a big man like Jerry. And as angry as Caitlin was, Aubrey had several inches on her too. They reluctantly climbed into the back seat. Jerry sat in the passenger seat and turned toward them. "And just in case you have any plans in mind, pass up your cell phones."

Caitlin pulled her phone from her pocket and handed it to him. She should have tried to call 911 earlier, but it had all happened so fast. Out of the corner of her eye, she saw Derek slide his phone between the seat cushions.

"Well?" Jerry said.

"I left mine at home," answered Derek. "My parents took away my screen time last week. Too much talking to strangers."

Caitlin tried to think about whether Derek had shown his phone to Aubrey since she'd picked them up, but he'd been in the back seat and she didn't think so.

"I haven't seen him with a phone," Aubrey said.

"You can search me if you want," said Derek.

"Fine." Jerry jerked down the sunshade so he could see them in the back seat through the mirror. "I'm watching you both. Not a word back there." He powered down Caitlin's phone and placed it in the glove box. Caitlin prayed that Derek had silenced his obnoxious ringtone.

They rode in silence as Aubrey turned up the mountain toward Monticello. They passed Michie Tavern and slowly rolled up to the Monticello's visitor entrance. A metal gate was lowered across the parking lot with a sign marked "Closed."

"Oh well, I guess we'll have to come back another time," said Derek.

"Quiet," Jerry snapped. "Keep going." He pointed further up the road to a narrow clearing in the trees just off the shoulder of the road. "Pull in there."

The tires crunched over the gravel and then came to a rest in a patch of pine needles. Aubrey killed the engine.

Jerry stepped from the car and opened the trunk. The sound of metal clanged behind them.

Aubrey opened the door and pulled the seat forward. "Everybody out."

Jerry slammed the trunk shut. He walked back to them with a thick pack over his shoulders that looked to be filled with tools. The crowbar was still in his hands.

"Let's go."

CHAPTER TWENTY-ONE

"Hello? Can you hear me?" Sam yelled into his phone, but Caitlin was only repeating his name. He ended the call in disgust and tried Derek, but his number went straight to voice mail. He'd sent them both text messages, but those still showed as undelivered. There must not be good cell service out by Poplar Forest. He didn't want to disturb Mom and Dad at the musical, or have to explain what Derek and Caitlin were really up to, but this was important. He tried their numbers too, but neither picked up.

His mind was racing.

Give me liberty or give me death.

That's what Aubrey's license plate meant. It could just be a coincidence, and the letters could stand for something else, or nothing at all, even, but Sam had stopped believing in coincidences with this mystery. Or at least not this many. There was only one person he knew of that would have a personalized plate like that. Jerry had been the premier actor in the region to portray Patrick Henry at both St. John's Church and Colonial Williamsburg before he was arrested. But what did Jerry have to do with Aubrey, and why would she have his car?

It didn't matter. He had to reach Derek and Caitlin.

He remembered that Mom had set Derek's and his phones to be trackable. When they'd first gotten their expensive new gadgets, she was convinced they'd lose them in a matter of days. She'd registered the whole family on a locator app. Sam pulled open the tracking app and selected Derek's name. It switched to a map screen, and he scrolled west toward Lynchburg and where Caitlin had said Poplar Forest was located. He found a town called Forest, but there was no dot showing Derek's location. How could that be? Was it not working?

He panned out to widen the map area and quickly saw a red dot appear above where he'd been looking. Derek's location was active, but he wasn't in Lynchburg. He was on Route 29, several miles north of where Poplar Forest should be. Sam watched for a minute as the red marker inched higher on the screen. Derek's phone was on the move. But where was he going? He followed Route 29 further north with his finger. It led straight to Charlottesville.

Why would they be going there? Had Jerry found them? There was no time. He had to do something.

He thought back to Dad's words in his bedroom. If he had an emergency, see Mr. Haskins. He had no idea how the old man could help matters, but this definitely qualified as an emergency. Sam bolted out the door and over to his neighbor's house, leaping onto the porch.

He banged on the door. "Mr. Haskins!"

A chair scraped against the floor inside.

Sam banged on the door again. "Mr. Haskins! Open up."

"I'm comin'," the old man hollered. "Keep your pants on, will ya?"

Sam started yelling before the door was fully open. "You have to help me." He was suddenly out of breath. "Derek and Caitlin. They're in trouble!"

Mr. Haskins gawked at him like he had two heads. "Hang on a cotton-pickin' minute, boy. I can't understand a word you're saying. Sit down and catch your breath before you fall down."

Sam shook his head. There wasn't time to sit down, but he tried to breathe.

"Derek and Caitlin are in trouble. We have to help them, but our parents are all downtown at the theater and they've turned their phones off. It's Jerry!"

Mr. Haskins raised his eyebrows. "What's that now? Who's Jerry? A friend of yours?"

Sam closed his eyes. This wasn't working. He had to get to Charlottesville. He looked down at the mulched flowerbeds and thought back to working in the garage. Then it came to him.

"Can you drive me somewhere?"

Mr. Haskins' mouth dropped open. "Me? On the road?"

Sam nodded. "It's an emergency, Mr. Haskins. It could be a matter of life and death."

"I haven't been on the highway in years." He patted his pants pocket and felt for his wallet. "Not sure if my license is even current anymore."

"Does your car still run?" asked Sam. He remembered it out in the garage, covered in dust.

Mr. Haskins frowned at him. "Does it run? Of course it runs, young man. I start her up once a month to keep the engine lubricated. Old habits die hard." He rubbed a few gray whiskers on his chin. "Say it's an emergency, eh?"

Sam began to reconsider his idea. Leaving Caitlin and Derek to fend for themselves might be less dangerous than riding with Mr. Haskins behind the wheel. "Maybe I should just wait for Mom and Dad to get back—"

"Let's do it!" Mr. Haskins waved an arm in the air like he was conducting an invisible orchestra.

"Are you sure?"

Mr. Haskins stared down at him. "You said your brother and girlfriend are in trouble, didn't ya?"

"Well, she's not my girlfriend…"

"Come on, boy. It's time to man up."

Sam exhaled. As usual, everything with Mr. Haskins was an odd ordeal. "Are you sure?"

"Why not? What's the worst that could happen?"

Sam gulped. That sounded like something Derek would say.

Mr. Haskins glanced over his shoulder. "Now I just have to find my keys…"

* * *

IT TOOK A FEW TRIES, but eventually the engine turned over and roared to life. Sam said a silent prayer as Mr. Haskins backed out of the garage and down the driveway into the cul-de-sac.

"What'd I tell ya!" the old man cackled. "Purrs like a kitten." He slapped Sam's leg. "Now, where are we headed on this rescue mission?" He was getting way too excited about things. Sam hoped he wouldn't have a heart attack. "Charlottesville," he answered.

"Charlottesville! Are we going to the university?"

Sam checked the tracking map on his phone. The red dot had come to a rest just outside Monticello. That must be where they were headed.

"Monticello."

Mr. Haskins grinned. "Now you're talkin', boy."

It was growing dark as they drove west into the mountains. Sam had just made this drive with his parents, but it seemed much longer now. When they'd started this adventure, he'd never dreamed that Jerry would be involved or that Derek and Caitlin would be in danger. He tried to imagine the connection between

Aubrey and Jerry, but ultimately it didn't matter. Whatever the link was, it had to be bad. He'd tried to reach both Derek and Caitlin several more times, but there was no answer to his calls or texts. What could they be doing? Sam knew he had to get to them.

A horn blared right behind them as Mr. Haskins made a sharp turn onto the highway. A huge eighteen-wheeler barreled by them.

"Are you okay?" asked Sam, gripping the seat. Despite how much noise this car engine was making, they were driving pretty slowly.

Mr. Haskins hunched over the steering wheel, staring out at the road. "Don't think that turn was there the last time I was out here."

Maybe this was a terrible idea.

"Reminds me of when I was courting the missus, back in the day."

"What?" asked Sam.

"When Julia and I started dating, she was a student."

Sam didn't really feel like making small talk, but if they were going to be in the car for an hour, they had to talk about something.

"At UVA?"

"Sort of."

"How could it be sort of? Either it is, or it isn't."

Mr. Haskins chuckled. "Well, she started out going to Mary Washington College—that was the school for girls. Then she transferred over to Virginia in 1970. She became one of the first women to live in a dorm on the Lawn."

"We saw those when we visited," said Sam. "They didn't allow women before that?"

"Not fully. Mostly just in nursing classes. Of course, things were different back then. Weren't a lot of black students either." He looked over at Sam across the seat. "Virginia hasn't always been the fastest to try new things, I'm afraid."

The tires passed over a rumble strip along the shoulder, and Mr. Haskins swung the wheel to get them back into the lane. Sam squeezed his seat tighter. "Maybe you should focus on the road."

Mr. Haskins laughed. "That's what Julia used to tell me too!"

Sam opened the tracking app again. The red dot was still at Monticello. Whatever they were doing, they'd stopped moving. He talked Mr. Haskins through directions from his phone to the exit off the highway.

"What are you planning to do when we get there?" asked Mr. Haskins.

Sam bit his lip. He'd been trying to figure that out himself. Without knowing what was really going on, all he could do was wing it. "Just warn them, I guess."

"About this Jerry fellow?"

"Right."

"If you need any backup, just flash me the signal. I'll give him the old one-two." He banged on the steering wheel, but then the engine began to sputter.

"Doggone it," Mr. Haskins muttered, as he pulled onto the shoulder halfway up the mountain. Sam recognized the sign for Michie Tavern just ahead that they'd seen when they'd visited Monticello.

"What's the matter?" asked Sam. "I thought you said you kept the engine all lubed?" They were so close. They couldn't stop now.

"I did, but I seem to have forgotten about one pesky detail."

"What?"

"Gas."

Sam closed his eyes. Oh, man.

"What are we going to do? I have to help them."

"Maybe someone will come along with some gas," said Mr. Haskins.

That could take forever. Sam looked out the window. Through the dusk, he could still see the old tavern that had been moved piece by piece. Monticello was just up the hill. He took a deep breath and turned to Mr. Haskins. "I'm walking the rest of the way."

"You sure?"

Sam nodded. "I have to get to them. There's no other choice."

They stepped out of the car and Mr. Haskins opened the trunk. He pulled out some flares and handed Sam a flashlight. "Here, you might need this."

"Thanks." Sam suddenly realized it might not be good to leave the old man sitting on the side of the road at night. "Will you be okay here?"

"Aw, I'll be fine. I was up in these mountains once on the Appalachian Trail with just a box of raisins when a storm rolled in for three days. Of course, that was probably forty years ago, but it takes more than a little gas shortage to keep this old guy down. Besides, I can use my secret weapon."

"The flares?"

Mr. Haskins grinned and pulled his wallet from his pocket. "Triple A! You mind if I borrow your phone?"

Sam didn't know why Mr. Haskins had AAA if he didn't drive, but he let him call for a service truck to bring him gas. When he finished, Mr. Haskins banged on the car hood. "I'll drive up and get you once I'm up and running." He gave Sam a serious glance. "Just be careful up there. It's dark."

"Okay, thanks," said Sam.

He turned and jogged up the steep, winding road. The air on the mountain was cool, and the forest was eerily quiet. He kept his light trained on the blacktop straight ahead of him, afraid to look into the trees. Were there bears in these woods? He tried not to think about what was lurking around him in the darkness.

Was this how Jack Jouett felt during his late-night ride to Charlottesville? Was he scared, riding for miles in the darkness? Sam wasn't exactly warning Thomas Jefferson that the British were coming, but warning Derek and Caitlin about Aubrey's connection to Jerry was important. Or what about Bobby Murcer at the plate after his good friend's emotional funeral? He guessed everybody had hard things they had to get through. Maybe this was one of his.

He tried to push back his doubts and his fears. He had to be brave. They were depending on him. He just hoped he wasn't too late.

CHAPTER TWENTY-TWO

W hen Sam finally reached the entrance to Monticello's parking lot, he bent over and caught his breath. The parking tiers were all vacant. The place was closed down for the night. He checked the tracking app. According to the map, he was right on top of Derek's phone. So where was he?

Sam turned and followed the road a few hundred feet up the hill. Suddenly he had moved past the dot. How could that be? He turned, walked back a few steps, and then stopped. It should be right here, but there was no parking lot, and the road was barren.

He shined the flashlight along the roadside. Maybe Derek's phone had dropped out of the window. Maybe he wasn't anywhere near Monticello. The light caught a reflection at the edge of the trees. A car was nestled into a small cutout on the shoulder. He moved his beam to the license plate.

GMLOGMD

It was them.

He snuck up and peered into the darkened windows. The car looked abandoned, but he had to be sure. Derek's phone must be stashed inside. Sam flashed his light across the seats, but they were bare. He knocked on the trunk gently just to make sure they weren't locked in, but everything was silent. Just in case, he dialed Caitlin's number again, but it still went right to voice mail. It was either turned off or out of battery. He switched his phone onto vibrate so it wouldn't make a sound if anyone called him back.

There was nothing left to do but head up the hill to the mansion. He skirted the visitor center, not wanting to run into any stray employees or lurking security guards. Whatever the reason that had brought Derek and Caitlin here, it was more likely they'd be at the mansion than the gift shop.

He worked his way up the wooded trail that led past the cemetery, turning off his flashlight as he passed the fence around the Jefferson family graves. The moon was a few days from full, but the sky was clear and Sam found his way easily. The gardens and outbuildings along Mulberry Row loomed in the shadows as Monticello neared on his left. So much had happened on this ground in the past. Perhaps hundreds of years ago there had been other moonlit walks like this one, undertaken by enslaved workers or even Jefferson himself.

He stepped onto the grass, moving stealthily in the

shadows from tree to tree. Now that he was here, he realized how little he'd thought things out. Sure, Aubrey's car was up the road, but Derek's phone was still in it. What had happened to everyone? Were they in the mansion on another tour? Was the building even open at night? Somehow Sam didn't think so. Just like everything else about this mystery, it would be too much of a coincidence.

Derek and Caitlin were here. So was Jerry.

He could feel it.

A flash of light caught his attention. It had come from the end of the closest wing that extended from the main house. Was that Derek and Caitlin, or was it Aubrey or Jerry? He had to be sure before he revealed himself. He pictured the layout in his mind—the main house had two narrow service wings stretching out on both sides like giant spider's legs. They'd ended their tour on the terrace next to the pavilion. That seemed to be where the light had come from.

He crept across the grass until he was close enough to see the pavilion in the darkness. The light flashed again, but it wasn't coming from the guesthouse at the pavilion. It had flashed from below the terrace, on the ground level. A muffled sound of metal hitting stone rang out, followed by a scraping. What were they doing? He had to get closer.

Sam slipped silently underneath the edge of the South Wing, next to the small historical display rooms. He pushed against the wall, trying to conceal himself in the shadows. He heard voices ahead, and he had a frightful feeling of déjà vu. This was just like meeting Jerry in the basement of St. John's. He suddenly wondered if he was ready to see the man that had for so long haunted his dreams. He pushed those thoughts away and inched forward to where he could see through the edge of the doorway. Sam recognized the tools lying around the room as similar to those the archaeologists had used at Jamestown. The area must be in the middle of an excavation.

Aubrey was holding a light, shining it against a narrow part of the far wall in the basement room. Sam felt a chill run down his spine. Jerry knelt on the floor, working a long metal crowbar. He'd already pried several bricks from the wall. Once, he stopped to glance at something on a phone before digging the crowbar back into the wall. They must have found another clue about the treasure. Was it here at Monticello and not at Poplar Forest? At this point, he didn't care what Jerry was digging for. The room was too small to hold Derek and Caitlin too. So where had they gone?

Sam carefully backed away from the pavilion room and then turned and jogged around the front of the house. He slipped down toward the passage below the North Wing, but as he turned the corner, he heard more voices and froze. Were Jerry and Aubrey working with others, or was it an echo from the digging on the other side of the house?

He leaned against the stone wall of the long, covered

passage and listened. There it was again. It sounded like… Derek?

He tiptoed into the covered passage. "Derek!" he half-whispered.

A voice answered back through the darkness. "Sam? Is that you?" It was Caitlin.

He ran forward, turning the corner near where they'd seen the icehouse. "Where are you?" he whispered.

"We're down here!" called Derek's voice.

Sam leaned down to the low, metal bars that protected the hole in the middle of the icehouse. He carefully shined his flashlight into the pit. He didn't want a flash of light to give him away the way it had Aubrey and Jerry. Ten feet below, Derek and Caitlin shielded their eyes from the light.

"What are you doing down there?"

"What are *you* doing up *there*?" Derek shot back.

"I'm trying to rescue you, stupid," Sam hissed. He studied the metal bars and wondered how the two of them had gotten stuck down there. He pulled on the bars and realized the lock was open. But the floor of the icehouse was too deep for them to be able to climb out.

"Sam, Jerry's here," called Caitlin.

"I know. I saw them over in the other wing. They're digging at bricks in the basement."

"He's Aubrey's father," she added.

Her father? That explained the license plate. Sam glanced back and forth to make sure no one was sneaking up behind him, but all seemed quiet. "Did you fall down there? How am I supposed to get you out?"

"He had a rope," said Derek. "He made us climb down, so we'd be out of the way. But he must have stashed it somewhere."

Sam felt all around the circular icehouse. He was afraid to turn on the flashlight again. It might attract attention. His foot stepped on a lump. He reached down and felt the prickly twine of a braided rope, like they had in gym class for climbing. He tugged it toward the top of the pit.

"I found it. Watch out. I'm dropping it down." He ran the rope through the door's iron bars for extra support and then tossed it into the dark hole. He pushed his feet against the stone exterior of the icehouse for leverage as Caitlin and Derek climbed out.

"Thanks," whispered Caitlin, pulling him into a hug. Sam dropped the rope and brushed his hands on his shorts. His palms were sore from the rough twine.

"How did you know we were here?" asked Derek.

"I followed your phone with the tracking app Mom made us download."

"Nice job," said Derek. "I hid it between the seats in Aubrey's car when Jerry forced us to come with them."

Sam nodded. "I figured out what her license plate meant. *Give me liberty or give me death.* That was when I realized Jerry must be connected. When you didn't answer my calls, I knew I had to warn you."

"I'm glad you came." Caitlin looked over her shoulder. "Where's your mom and dad?"

"I couldn't reach them either. They're with your parents at the play downtown, remember?"

Derek looked confused. "Then how'd you get here?"

Sam grimaced, thinking about how he'd left his elderly neighbor stranded on the side of the road. He hoped he was okay. "Mr. Haskins drove me."

"What?" exclaimed Derek.

"Shh!" said Sam. "They'll hear you."

"Where is he?" Caitlin whispered.

"We ran out of gas at Michie Tavern, so I ran the rest of the way. He's still with the car." Sam leaned around the corner of the icehouse. The corridor was still dark and quiet. "But why did they bring you here? I thought you were going to Poplar Forest."

"The treasure is in the South Pavilion," said Caitlin. "We realized the map was for the original kitchen here at Monticello, not the one at Poplar Forest. So we were on our way here when Jerry called and met us at a rest stop."

"You mean they were planning this the whole time?" Sam asked.

"I'm not sure," said Caitlin. "But whatever they're doing, we need to get out of here."

"What about the treasure?" asked Derek.

A sound on the stones caught their attention. Sam spun around to find Jerry standing at the edge of the passage, the metal crowbar in his hand.

"Well, well, well," he cackled. "Look who decided to join the party."

CHAPTER TWENTY-THREE

"Run!" shouted Derek, pushing past Jerry toward the basement passageway.

Sam grabbed Caitlin's hand and followed his brother into the darkness, his heart beating as loudly in his chest as the sounds of their steps on the stone floor as Jerry chased close behind.

They reached the end of the passage and realized their mistake. The wooden door into the basement was locked. There was nowhere else to go. Derek kicked it hard with his foot once, but it didn't budge. A second kick cracked the frame enough to push it open. Sam cringed at the destruction, but he didn't think the door was original. Either way, it was easier to replace a door than his head after Jerry hit him with a crowbar.

They dashed behind Derek into the open doorway of the wine cellar. Wide, wooden barrels were stacked against one wall. A long rack of glass bottles was against the opposite wall. They leaped over the protective railing and crouched down out of view behind a stack of barrels. It was cool and quiet in the basement, but they were running out of places to go. This was way too much like hiding from Jerry beneath one of the old church pews at St. John's. Caitlin reached over and squeezed Sam's hand. He wondered if she was thinking the same thing. How had they gotten in this position again?

Jerry's steps paused at the doorway. He stepped onto the wooden boards of the elevated landing. "You can't hide forever. I'm at the end of my patience with you three. I should have at least gotten rid of the two of you back at the car when I had the chance. You can thank my daughter for allowing you to get this far."

Sam glimpsed him between the barrels. Jerry raised his leg up over the railing and stepped down to the cellar floor. Derek nudged Sam's arm and motioned to him and Caitlin to position their hands and feet against the closest wooden barrel, bracing their backs against the wall. Sam didn't know if these barrels were empty or filled with wine, but as Jerry stepped in front of the row of barrels, it was their only chance for a diversion. Their only chance to get away.

"Now!" Derek grunted, and they heaved on the barrel. It lurched forward, crashing into two more and rolling right into Jerry, knocking him against the far wall.

Derek jumped up and scrambled back into the hallway with Sam and Caitlin close behind. But right outside the door was Aubrey, a dark wooden crate in her arms.

"Hey!" she exclaimed, as Derek pushed by her and ran down the passage toward the icehouse. She recovered and blocked the way before Sam and Caitlin could follow.

"This way," Sam called, turning the other direction. They ran straight across the basement toward the other passage that led to the South Wing. Sam braced himself to kick at the door, but from the inside, it opened easily.

"We have to hide," said Sam, as they ran to the end of the South Wing. He didn't know where Derek had headed, but he hoped he had gotten away. Caitlin ducked into a dark room and crouched along the wall. As Sam followed her into the shadows, he realized where they were. They were in the basement of the South Pavilion, where Jerry and Aubrey had been digging.

"Look!" he whispered, pointing to the back wall.

"They found it?"

Sam shined his flashlight toward the place he had seen Jerry digging. Red bricks were scattered along the floor under a jagged, empty space in the middle of the wall. Two dark wooden crates, like the one Aubrey had been carrying outside the wine cellar, sat next to the bricks.

Caitlin paused, glancing over her shoulder. The lawn seemed quiet, so she inched forward and pulled back the top of the first crate. She gasped as a silver serving tray and candlestick glistened in the light.

The treasure.

She moved to the second crate, pulling back the top to reveal pieces of straw. She reached past the straw, scattering what looked like shelled corn down onto the bricks. She pulled a cloth wrapping from the crate and then slowly undid the covering to reveal a creased, rectangular leather object.

"Books…" she whispered, pulling back the straw again to reveal a dozen small, leather-bound volumes. "Jefferson's collection!"

Of course he would have hidden books. Now it all made sense.

Sam jumped as his phone buzzed in his pocket, but a wave of relief swept over him when he saw his dad's name on the screen. He tapped and whispered an answer. "Dad?"

"Sam, we just got your text." His dad's voice sounded strained. "Where are you?"

"We're at Monticello. You have to help us."

"Monticello?" Dad exclaimed. "How did you—never mind. Are Derek and Caitlin with you?"

"Yes," Sam answered. "But Dad…" His voice cracked, and he suddenly felt tears well up in his eyes. "I'm so sorry."

"What is it, Sam? Are you safe?"

Caitlin put her hand on his arm reassuringly. Sam took a breath. "Jerry's here, Dad. He's after us. But we're hiding."

"We're on our way," Dad said. "Can you stay out of sight?"

Caitlin's fingers dug sharply into Sam's arm as a shadow stretched across the grass from the corner of the pavilion.

"I gotta go, Dad," he whispered. "Please hurry." He stuffed the phone back in his pocket and crept to the doorway. It wouldn't do any good for Dad to rescue him if he was already dead.

"We have to get out of here," whispered Caitlin, "or we'll be trapped again."

Sam nodded, and they both stepped toward the door. Aubrey stood in front of the next room. They jumped up and ran, but Sam tripped over something in the grass and flew forward. He splashed into a pool of cool water, and he struggled to hold his breath while he flailed and kicked. It was Jefferson's fishpond, and he'd run right into it. Sam found his footing and lunged back toward the grass, but he'd made a lot of noise in the process. He wiped the water from his eyes and tried to look around. Where had Caitlin gone? Was Aubrey still—

"That's far enough," a voice growled.

Sam turned around to see Jerry and Aubrey standing behind him with Caitlin securely in Jerry's clutches. Water dripped from his hair as he stepped back onto the grass. How could he have been such a klutz? Now it was really over.

Jerry pulled out a thin section of rope and cut it into

pieces with a pocketknife. "I should have done this to begin with."

He tied Sam's and Caitlin's hands together behind their backs and then tied the bindings together too. Their feet were free, but they'd never be able to run very far tied back to back. Sam glanced around the darkness hoping to see Derek, but the lawn was empty.

Jerry seemed to have the same thought. "Unless you want things to get much worse for these two, I suggest you show yourself immediately!"

It was quiet for a moment, but then Derek stepped out from the trees. He carried the crate that Aubrey had been holding in the passageway and set it in the grass. "Sorry guys," he said, raising his hands in surrender.

Jerry secured Derek to the ropes that held Sam and Caitlin. Aubrey pulled a wheelbarrow from the garden and loaded up the three wooden crates and their tools. Jerry shoved the prisoners past the buildings on Mulberry Row and down to the small pavilion in the gardens. He tied the rope to a bar on the floor until he was satisfied they couldn't pull loose.

"I hope you're happy, Aubrey," Caitlin shouted. "I was right. You're still nothing but a thief."

"We have everything we need," said Aubrey, pulling the wheelbarrow to the pavilion. "Let's get out of here."

"One moment," Jerry replied, moving to the doorway. He pulled an object from his pocket. There was a clicking sound. Then a faint orange glow illuminated his face. Jerry's lips curved into an evil grin. "As soon as we clean up these loose ends."

"What are you doing?" shouted Derek.

Sam realized what Jerry was planning to do with the lighter. "Oh my gosh…"

"You're crazy!" Caitlin shrieked.

Aubrey stood in the doorway, her mouth open and her wide eyes staring.

Jerry's expression was wild. "This all ends now."

"Aubrey!" Caitlin shouted. "Don't just stand there, do something!"

Aubrey got past her initial shock and stepped toward them. "Dad, no! They're just kids. We have what we need. Let's go."

"Great idea," he answered, dropping the flaming lighter. It landed in a wicker basket filled with clumps of white cotton and cloth blankets. Immediately, the flame began to spread through the basket.

Sam, Derek and Caitlin lurched away from the flaming basket as far as their rope would allow.

A look of horror filled Aubrey's face. "This wasn't the plan, Daddy!"

Jerry shook his head and walked through the doorway as a tuft of smoke began to rise from the basket. Flickering shadows reflected against the windowpanes of the pavilion as flames grew in the corner of the room. "Neither was my going to prison."

"This isn't who you are," cried Aubrey, her eyes filling with tears. "We were trying to find history, not destroy it." She stared at the three prisoners huddled against the wall. "And definitely not kill innocent kids!"

"Innocent?" Jerry bellowed. He turned back to them from the doorway. His evil grin had changed to determined resignation. "You don't understand what they did to me, Aubrey. What they did to our family. It drove you and your mother away from me when they sent me to prison. They took everything."

Aubrey grabbed his arm. "No, Daddy, you took all that from yourself. This is not the answer to anything."

Jerry shook away her grasp. He stared through the darkness into the valley and then glared back at her in disgust. "I have what I came for. I thought you were different, Aubrey, but you're just like your mother. You'll never understand." He turned and lifted the wheelbarrow handles, striding off into the darkness.

CHAPTER TWENTY-FOUR

A ubrey stood motionless as she watched her father wheel the treasure into the night.

"He left me," she whispered, almost as if to herself.

"Aubrey!" Derek shouted. "Do something. Get us out of here!"

Sam, Derek, and Caitlin strained against the ropes, but Jerry had tied them in endless knots. The flames grew higher in the corner of the Garden Pavilion, leaping from the basket to the walls and window frames. Sam could feel the heat building against his skin. Once the wooden frame caught, the entire structure would go up in flames.

Finally, Aubrey turned back to them. Her shock at the sight made it seem as though she'd forgotten all about them and the fire. She jumped toward them and tried to undo the ropes, but they were tied too tightly. Then she spun and bolted through the doorway.

"Aubrey?" yelled Caitlin, as she disappeared into the darkness. "Come back!"

"What are we going to do?" Sam cried. "I don't want to die in Thomas Jefferson's flaming garden house!"

"I'm open to ideas," said Caitlin, still straining to pull loose.

"I don't know," said Derek, "but if we don't get out of here soon, we're going to be a permanent part of history."

Suddenly Aubrey reappeared in the doorway.

"You came back!" exclaimed Sam.

She held a pair of pruning clippers in her hand. "Pull the ropes taut and then hold still," she ordered, reaching behind them to get at the ropes. But as the others leaned forward, it put Sam's face closer to the flames. He grimaced at the heat against his face. It felt like his eyebrows were singed already.

"Almost got it," said Aubrey. She clipped through the final strand, releasing their arms and nearly sending them tumbling into the fire.

All four of then ran out of the pavilion just as several panes of glass shattered and the flames leapt up through the windows, toward the wooden lattice railing on the roof.

"How do we put it out?" cried Caitlin.

"I think it's too late," said Derek.

Sam looked around. They were far enough from the other buildings that he didn't think the fire would spread past the corner of the garden, but there wasn't any water other than the fishpond where he'd splashed down earlier, and there was no way to bring that to the pavilion.

"Are you all okay?" asked Aubrey, visibly shaken. She looked like she was about to fall over.

"Oh sure," said Derek. "We're just great. Other than almost being burned alive by your lunatic father, we're in tip-top shape."

Aubrey sat in the grass and shook her head. "I don't know what happened. I've never seen him like that before. It's like something snapped. I thought he'd be different after his release, but maybe his anger only hardened during his time in prison."

Another window frame collapsed inward and the entire structure was filled with flames. They all moved out of the garden to the edge of Mulberry Row. Sam stared down the trail but didn't see any sign of Jerry. He was probably at the car by that point.

Headlights glinted against the windows of the mansion, and a truck sped around the corner. It swung right onto the trail along Mulberry Row, skidding to a stop in front of the gardens where they stood.

Aubrey jumped up and, for a moment, looked as though she might make a run for it, but Derek quickly stepped in front of her. "Don't even think about it."

She sank back to the grass and lowered her head into her arms.

A woman with glasses jumped out of the truck. Initially, she just stared at the flaming pavilion, her face aghast, like she was dreaming. When a police car charged up the hill behind her, she turned to the four kids in the grass. "What happened to the Garden Pavilion? Are you all okay? What are you doing here?"

The flashing lights of the police car filled the grounds with color. Both doors opened, and one officer stood and shouted into his radio while another ran toward the kids. They both appeared to recognize that the pavilion was past saving, even as another siren rang out in the distance.

The third car that came up the trail had a racing stripe across the side panel. Mr. Haskins opened his door and slowly stood from the driver's seat. Like the first woman with the glasses, Mr. Haskins stared in amazement at the blaze. "Holy mackerel...," he muttered, his face a mixture of fascination and fear.

Sam waved and ran over to his neighbor, glad to see that he'd made it after being left at the side of the road.

"You kids okay?" Mr. Haskins asked.

"I think so," answered Sam.

"That your handiwork?" Mr. Haskins pointed at the smoldering Garden Pavilion.

"No, that was Jerry."

"Did ya give 'im the old one-two?"

Sam shook his head. "Not really. And he got away with the treasure."

One of the police officers called Sam over to where Derek and Caitlin still sat with Aubrey. He asked them lots of questions about what had happened, eyeing Aubrey carefully as her part in the events came out. When they'd all finished, he ordered her to her feet, slapping handcuffs on her wrists just in case she had any plans of sneaking away. The officer spoke into his radio to put out an APB for Jerry in the blue coupe with the GMLOGMD plate.

The woman with the glasses, who turned out to be Dr. Monroe, the head curator of Monticello, pulled Sam, Derek, and Caitlin aside to learn more about what had happened. They took turns sharing what they'd seen in the crates when they were in the basement of the South Pavilion, how they'd found the drawing of the secret fireplace compartment behind the loose brick in the Cuddy, and the original journal and letter from the granddaughters. Dr. Monroe stared back at them incredulously as they spoke. At first, Sam thought maybe Dr. Monroe wouldn't believe them, but after she went and inspected the open space in the wall below the South Pavilion, she came back and peppered them with dozens of questions.

"You mean, all this started from one of the books you took from my garage?" asked Mr. Haskins. He seemed to be nearly as amazed as Dr. Monroe.

"That's right," said Derek. "You should clean it out more often."

The fire truck pulled to a stop beside the gardens, and despite the pavilion being charred beyond repair, they hosed it down just to keep the flames from spreading to any other part of the property. A few minutes later, a message came across the radio that a squad car had picked Jerry up as he was driving down the south side of the mountain. And based on the information that Derek and Caitlin had provided, they'd also found his other car at the rest stop several miles away.

Some time later, the officers were notified that both Sam and Derek's and Caitlin's parents were at the entrance by the visitor center, and they were allowed to drive up to join the crowd that was now assembled in front of Mr. Jefferson's house. A few minutes after that, yet another police car arrived, this time with Jerry cuffed in the back seat.

Sam was glad when the officers didn't let Jerry out of the squad car. He didn't want to hear anything else the man had to say. He knew Jerry would be furious, but maybe now he'd be locked up for a very long time. Sam didn't know the penalty for burning down part of a national treasure like Monticello, but it had to be major. And attempted murder wouldn't look good either.

When the parents and kids were reunited, there were several moments of warm hugs and stern looks. Mrs. Murphy recognized Aubrey from when she'd bought the books at her store. And the boys' mom and dad couldn't believe that Mr. Haskins had driven Sam all the way up to Monticello at night.

The officer who'd picked up Jerry called Dr. Monroe over to his squad car. The officer opened his trunk and pulled out four crates. They watched Dr. Monroe take a half-step back and rest her hand on her forehead.

"Wait a minute," said Derek. "They just pulled four crates out of the trunk. Didn't Jerry only leave with three in the wheelbarrow? What gives?"

Sam glanced back at Aubrey on the grass, but she only shook her head and looked away.

"Do you think there was more?" asked Caitlin, as Dr. Monroe and the officer carried the crates up to near where they stood.

"Come on," said Derek. "Let's see."

"Boys," called Dad, "be careful and don't get in the way of the officers."

"You found the book collection," said Caitlin.

"And the treasure," said Sam.

Caitlin turned and frowned at him. "They're both treasures, Sam." She turned back to Dr. Monroe. "Am I right?"

She nodded. "Without question, Caitlin." She gently reached into the first crate and pulled back the cloth to reveal a small, old, leather-bound book. Sam heard her take a short breath. "A petit," she muttered.

"Is that good?" asked Derek.

Dr. Monroe looked through the book and nodded. "Jefferson kept a personal collection of smaller format books which he called his petit-format collection. We believed it was mostly kept at Poplar Forest, but this seems to be a box of additional volumes of poetry... Italian, French, and Latin."

"Are they valuable?" asked Sam.

"Anything from Jefferson's collection is valuable," Dr. Monroe replied, as she looked through the second crate of books and then pulled a gleaming silver candlestick from the third crate. "Oh, this is stunning!"

"Holy mackerel!" Mr. Haskins came up behind them and placed a hand on Sam's shoulder. "Don't you dare tell me that those beauties were in my garage too."

Derek pointed at the final crate. "Where did that one come from? We only saw them take away three from the basement."

Dr. Monroe opened the top carefully. "The officer said this was in the car that was parked at the rest area. The man apparently had it hidden in his trunk."

Sam glanced at Caitlin and Derek in surprise. Why would Jerry have another crate hidden in his trunk? Had he been here before? Had he stolen things from other places?

Dr. Monroe gasped as she pulled out another leather-bound volume.

"Aw," moaned Derek. "Just more books?"

"That's not a petit, is it?" asked Caitlin. She was right —it was larger than the others.

Dr. Monroe reached in for several more books, her face growing more excited as she went. She stopped and looked up at them in astonishment. "I can't believe it."

CHAPTER TWENTY-FIVE

"This is great. I'm always traveling by train from now on," exclaimed Derek as they walked through the crowd of busy commuters on the Amtrak platform. Mrs. Murphy directed them to follow the flow of people until they emerged into the cavernous central room of Washington DC's Union Station. The ceiling arched high above them, decorated with hundreds of octagon-shaped tiles. It was awesome, and it reminded Sam of when Mom and Dad had walked them through the train stations in Philadelphia and New York.

"Which way?" asked Sam, as they walked outside and across a busy street that was bustling with traffic.

Caitlin pointed ahead of them. "Don't you see anything familiar?"

He glanced up and saw the dome of the US Capitol building poking above the trees. "Wow, we're close." He remembered exploring the Capitol and the White House during their last adventure that had concluded at Mount Vernon.

"Think I should swing by the Oval Office first?"

"Not today, Derek," said Mrs. Murphy. "I think the Library of Congress will keep us busy enough."

The fourth crate that the police had found in the trunk of Jerry's car had turned out to be pretty important. Aubrey explained to the officers that before her father had gone to prison, he'd been in the middle of a worldwide search for the remaining "lost" books from Thomas Jefferson's personal collection. Just as their Monticello tour guide had described, Jefferson had sold his library to replace the Library of Congress, which had been burned by the British during the War of 1812, and another fire on Christmas Eve in 1851 destroyed two-thirds of what he'd sold them.

Using whatever means necessary, Jerry had been determined to find the elusive volumes. Once Dr. Monroe had analyzed the books they'd discovered beneath the South Pavilion and the new batch that Jerry had been collecting, she loaned them to the Library of Congress for display in their special Jefferson Library exhibit. The silver candlesticks and other treasures would go on display at Monticello and in other museums related to Jefferson.

Sam didn't know if Jerry had been honestly collecting the rare books or if he'd stolen them like he seemed to do most of the time. Either way, it was exciting that they were going to be displayed in the Library of Congress. Sam just hoped that after all the fires there, they'd finally invested in a good sprinkler system.

"This is a library?" asked Derek, as they walked into a huge stone building across the street from the Capitol. "It looks like a palace."

"A palace for books," said Caitlin.

Dr. Monroe was waiting for them inside, just past security. "You made it! Welcome to the largest library in the world." She handed them each a special visitor's badge. "Over 168 million items in all."

"Holy cow," muttered Derek. "That's a lot of books."

Dr. Monroe smiled. "Yes it is. In fact, it takes up three different buildings: the oldest being the Thomas Jefferson building, followed by the John Adams building, and then most recently the James Madison building."

The area called the Great Hall looked very much like a palace, with tall white marble columns, staircases, and stained glass and artwork in the tall ceiling.

"This is amazing," said Caitlin, staring all around. "But can we see the Jefferson exhibit? I'm so excited."

"Absolutely," replied Dr. Monroe. "But first, I know you'll want to see our crown jewel."

Derek's eyes opened wide. "You have jewels?"

Dr. Monroe laughed. "I mean our Main Reading Room. It's one of the most amazing rooms in the world."

"The world?" repeated Sam. That sounded like a bit

of an exaggeration. He'd seen a lot of fancy rooms, like at the Jefferson Hotel, the Rotunda at the Capitol, and they'd even been in the Oval Office. How great could a library be?

Dr. Monroe led them up a staircase to a balcony that overlooked a large room. As the tour group ahead of them moved aside, the four of them stepped up to the railing.

"Oh my gosh…." Sam grabbed hold of the railing to steady himself.

Dr. Monroe wasn't kidding. It was truly the most amazing room he'd ever seen. The balcony faced a gigantic space that looked too good to be real, like it was a painting from someone's imagination. High above them was an ornate dome that seemed just as grand as the Rotunda in the Capitol. Beneath it were series after series of intricate arched windows, columns, statues, and artwork. On the floor was a circular pattern of wooden tables and desks, each with a glowing white reading lamp.

"I don't even know what to say," muttered Mrs. Murphy, dumbfounded.

"It takes your breath away, doesn't it?" said Dr. Monroe. "While it's not the most visited destination in our nation's capital, it might be the most beautiful."

"I could stand here and look at this room all day," said Caitlin.

"Are the Jefferson books in here?" asked Sam, breaking free of the room's trance.

"No, they're on display in their own special room,"

Dr. Monroe answered. "Come on, I'll show you." She led them down the hall to a smaller room that featured one long, connected display rack that curved like a letter "c" and wrapped around the center of the room.

"I cannot live without books." Sam read from a panel introducing the space which called it "Thomas Jefferson's Library."

Caitlin stepped into the opening of the "c." "It's bookshelves!"

Inside rested row after row of antique-looking books set behind protective glass. The shelves were arranged into sections called Memory, Reason, and Imagination.

"Which ones are ours?" asked Derek, gazing up and down the shelves.

"They're not ours," Sam reminded him.

"They belong to history," said Caitlin.

Derek shook his head. "You know what I mean. The ones from the secret passage and that Jerry had in his trunk."

"There are several types of books in the exhibit," said Dr. Monroe. She unlocked one of the glass cases and carefully pulled out a book. She turned to the inside cover and pointed to some faint writing. "See that letter 'J'? That indicates that this was one of Jefferson's original volumes. They're marked with green ribbons."

Sam scanned the displays and saw many thin green ribbons sticking up from the leather books. "There's a lot of them."

Dr. Monroe nodded. "About two thousand of his

originals remain. The books with gold ribbons are replacement copies of the same title, but not the actual book owned by Jefferson."

"Wow…," muttered Caitlin.

Derek pointed to several white, rectangular shapes that were scattered across the shelves. "What are those?"

"The white boxes are titles that are missing. From records, we know they were books that Jefferson sold to Congress; however, we've been unable to locate the original or any copy." Dr. Monroe grinned. "But today we're chipping away at that number." She slid over a rolling book cart, pulling out one of the books that Jerry had found. She reached into the shelf, removed one of the white boxes, and then turned to Caitlin. "Would you like the honor?"

Caitlin squeaked out a gasp, her face looking like it was about to burst. "Oh my gosh! I'd love to." She took the worn leather book and a green ribbon from Dr. Monroe, placed the ribbon inside the book's cover, and then set it in the open space on the shelf.

Sam had to admit, it was pretty sweet.

"There, another piece of the puzzle has been filled in," proclaimed Dr. Monroe. "Remember, these are not just books. They are words and ideas that helped shape our new country and which informed Thomas Jefferson as he penned great works, like the Declaration of Independence, that forever changed our world."

"Can I try one?" asked Derek.

Dr. Monroe nodded. "Of course. That's why you're here."

"Thank you for letting us be a part of this," gushed Mrs. Murphy as she took a turn replacing one of the white boxes on the shelves.

After they'd finished and said goodbye to Dr. Monroe, they walked back outside. "Send me those pictures you took, Mom," said Caitlin. "I want to send one to Linda back at Poplar Forest since she helped us find the kitchen."

"We should send one to all the people who helped us," said Derek. "Like Martha and the other lady at the UVA library, and John, our guide at Monticello."

"Don't forget about Mr. Haskins," said Sam. "You guys would probably still be stuck down in that icehouse if he hadn't driven me."

"I know one person who won't be getting a picture," said Caitlin.

"Jerry?" said Derek. "We should send him one. He could use it to decorate his cell."

"No, thank you," said Sam, quickly. The last thing he wanted was to give Jerry any more reasons to think about them. One collect call with a warning from prison was enough.

"I was talking about Aubrey," said Caitlin.

"Oh, right," said Derek.

"What do you think is going to happen to her, anyway?" asked Sam.

Caitlin shrugged. "I don't know. Do you, Mom?"

"I haven't heard," Mrs. Murphy answered. "I'm sure she'll be facing consequences, but my suspicion is that the prosecutor may give her some sympathy since most of her actions seemed to be orchestrated by her father. I feel bad for her."

"Don't," said Caitlin. "She doesn't deserve it."

"People make mistakes, honey. And when it really mattered, she did the right thing. Hopefully that girl is young enough that she'll learn from her mistakes and make better decisions down the road." Mrs. Murphy put her hand on Caitlin's shoulder. "Just like some other people I know."

Caitlin sighed. "I'm sorry again. I shouldn't have lied and snuck off without telling you. I guess we're all walking contradictions in our own way."

They turned the corner and headed back toward Union Station. "Do you know another thing that I read was super important to Thomas Jefferson?" asked Caitlin.

"You mean besides books, domes, and skylights?" Sam shook his head. "What?"

"Ice cream! He brought the recipes over from France." Caitlin stopped and pointed at a soft-serve truck parked on the curb. Sam's mouth started to water at the sight.

"Hey, Mrs. Murphy," Derek said with a grin. "What do ya say? Wanna buy us all a treat? Thomas Jefferson would have wanted you to."

"Hmm." She stopped and put her hand to her chin.

"Do you think you can be nice to Sam for the rest of the trip, including the train ride home?"

Derek rolled his eyes dramatically and then laughed. "You drive a hard bargain, but you have a deal."

Sam smiled. Sweet.

ACKNOWLEDGMENTS

I knew early on that I wanted to write a book about Thomas Jefferson, even though I'd touched on him in themes from Book Two, *Mystery on Church Hill*. Similar to writing about George Washington, there are so many angles from which to tackle Jefferson, but I was intrigued by the lesser-known story about the British seizing Richmond and attacking Charlottesville in an attempt to capture the departing Virginia governor and legislature. The story of Jack Jouett's late-night ride and warning was one my kids had learned in school, but wasn't widely known outside of Virginia.

During my research, I discovered the vast resources of letters that had been preserved and connected to Jefferson and his family. Correspondence between Jefferson's granddaughters caught my eye, particularly as I learned of their close relationship. With two exceptions, the words "quoted" from letters between the sisters in this book are imagined, however they were inspired and constructed from my reading and study of many actual Jefferson family letters, including their style of greetings and closing salutations. Most of the excerpt in Chapter Four that describes the Cuddy was lifted from a letter written from another of Jefferson's granddaughters, Virginia Randolph (Trist) to her future husband, Nicholas Trist on June 5, 1823. In addition, the touching excerpt in the chapter on Poplar Forest by Ellen Randolph is a direct quotation, which I thought perfectly conveyed the relationship the sisters had with their grandfather. The Library of Congress has great online access to this and many of the Jefferson family letters if you're interested in reading more.

I first visited the Library of Congress last year during my research for Book Seven, *Spies at Mount Vernon*. While it didn't fit into that story, the incredible Main Reading Room is truly one of the most amazing places I've ever visited. I was fascinated by the story of the British burning the library during the War of 1812, of Jefferson's sale of his books to replace it, and the subsequent fire which destroyed much of that replacement. When I found an article about how the LOC staff had stealthily been piecing the contents of Jefferson's books back together over the past decade (most of which, as hard as it was for this New York Giants fan to hear, came largely from a donation from Dallas Cowboys owner Jerry Jones), I knew I'd found part of an exciting mystery storyline.

The opportunity to learn from the past has always been something that's drawn me to history, and every figure in history is by definition complex because they, like all of us today, are individuals. While I don't think these mystery books are the proper format in which to hammer away at deep social issues, I make a conscious effort to address them lightly, even delicate ones like Jefferson's relationship with Sally Hemings, in a hope that families and teachers can address them in the way that best fits what's appropriate for the age of the reader. For history to teach best, I believe we must acknowledge its beauty and ugliness alike, so that we might continue to seek a more perfect union.

Two books I leaned heavily on in my early research of Jefferson were Pulitzer Prize-winner *Thomas Jefferson: The Art of Power* by Jon Meacham, and *Flight from Monticello*, by Michael Kranish, both of which were highly engaging and I'd highly recommend. I borrowed the title concept from Mr. Kranish and I hope he'll indulge me, as our books are wildly different. Thanks go out to a number of people at the different historical sites I visited during my research—including some that didn't make it into the final version of the story like Jefferson's boyhood home at Tuckahoe Plantation (but I'm including it in a companion short story), and Natural Bridge, which Jefferson purchased from the King of England. Many thanks to the staff at Monticello, including Linnea Grim, and Andrew Miles, who led an excellent "Behind the Scenes" tour that included the Dome Room and Cuddy.

Thank you to Ginny for a great tour at Poplar Forest, and to the helpful ladies working at Albert and Shirley Small Special Collections Library at The University of Virginia.

Some plot points come easier than others, and this was likely the hardest book so far for me to finish in The Virginia Mysteries. In fact, I decided to take a break after writing the first third of the book and concentrate on a new sci-fi series called *Final Kingdom*. But it was waiting for me several months later and as is often the case, talking out some points with a friend as a sounding board was very helpful. One of the best things about writing multiple books is that I've established a trusted team that keeps these books as strong as possible. Thanks to my editor, Kim Sheard, proofreader from Polgarus Studio Stephanie Parent, and cover designer from ebooklaunch.com, Dane Low. Thank you to Ali for her listening and plot ideas, my wife Mary for her first reader pass, the many booksellers and librarians who help get these books into the hands of young readers, and my awesome advance reader team.

Mary, Matthew, Josh, and Aaron, your love and support makes this all worthwhile. And to an ever-growing number of readers, young and old, I hope you continue to enjoy these stories as much as I love making them. You're the best.

ABOUT THE AUTHOR

Steven K. Smith is the author of *The Virginia Mysteries*, *Brother Wars*, and *Final Kingdom* series for middle grade readers. He lives with his wife, three sons, and a golden retriever in Richmond, Virginia.

For more information, visit:

www.stevenksmith.net

Email: steve@myboys3.com

Facebook & Instagram: @stevenksmithauthor

Twitter: @stevenksmith1

ALSO BY STEVEN K. SMITH

The Virginia Mysteries:

Summer of the Woods
Mystery on Church Hill
Ghosts of Belle Isle
Secret of the Staircase
Midnight at the Mansion
Shadows at Jamestown
Spies at Mount Vernon
Escape from Monticello
Pictures at the Protest
Pirates on the Bay

Brother Wars Series:

Brother Wars
Cabin Eleven
The Big Apple

Final Kingdom Trilogy (Ages 10+)

The Missing
The Recruit
The Bridge

DID YOU ENJOY ESCAPE FROM MONTICELLO?

WOULD YOU ... REVIEW?

Online reviews are crucial for indie authors like me. They help bring credibility and make books more discoverable by new readers. No matter where you purchased your book, if you could take a few moments and give an honest review at *Amazon* or *Goodreads*, I'd be grateful.

If you're a teacher, be sure to check out the reading comprehension quiz, in-person and virtual classroom visit opportunities, historical links, and other materials on my website at stevenksmith.net.

Made in United States
North Haven, CT
18 June 2022

20379957R00136